SAVING MOZART

Raphaël Jerusalmy

SAVING MOZART
THE DIARY OF OTTO J. STEINER

*Translated from the French
by Howard Curtis*

Europa
editions

Europa Editions
214 West 29th Street
New York, N.Y. 10001
www.europaeditions.com
info@europaeditions.com

Copyright © 2012 by Actes Sud
First Publication 2013 by Europa Editions

Translation by Howard Curtis
Original title: *Sauver Mozart. Le journal d'Otto J. Steiner*
Translation copyright © 2013 by Europa Editions

Library of Congress Cataloging in Publication Data is available
ISBN 978-1-60945-145-5

Jerusalmy, Raphaël
Saving Mozart

Book design by Emanuele Ragnisco
www.mekkanografici.com

Cover photo © mladn61/iStock

Prepress by Grafica Punto Print – Rome

Printed in the USA

To the memory of Jacques Eisenband
(Paris, 12 December 1936—Auschwitz, early March 1944)

SAVING MOZART

Diary of Otto J. Steiner

(July 1939—August 1940)

F riday 7 July 1939

I hate Fridays. Fillet of cod and boiled potatoes. The custodian's son went to buy me half a pound of saveloy on the quiet. I feast on it in my room. Outside, it's gray, with a dull light.

I never kept a diary in the old days. I'm not sure it's such a good idea now.

*

I put a Caruso record on the phonograph just before my afternoon nap. Keeping the volume down. *Vesti la giubba e la faccia infarina, la gente paga, e rider vuole qua . . .* It's the best recording. Not at all nasal. The needle glides over the grooves, caresses the wax. The horn vibrates but Caruso's voice stays firm.

My chest hurts. It makes the whole upper part of my body feel tight, like cramp.

Sunday 16 July 1939

It's Sunday. It's been a bad week. From every point of view. But today, the courtyard is filled with radiant sunlight.

The preparations for the festival are in full swing. I'd

love to take a walk as far as the Festspielhaus. But I don't
know if my lungs will hold out.

*

What a wonderful day! I had a drink by the river. The
surface of the Salzach rippled in the breeze. The white
wine went to my head. I didn't have the strength to go all
the way to the old town. The fronts of the houses are
already covered in flags that flap in the wind. They say the
Führer is going to put in a brief appearance. He may even
attend one of the concerts.

Tuesday 25 July 1939
Hans came to see me. He brought me some tickets.
He's adamant that I make an effort. Two or three articles.
The coming festival has put new life into me. The medi-
cines knock me out. I threw them in the garbage cans next
to the kitchens. Without anybody seeing me.

After Hans left, I went down to the dayroom to have a
cup of tea. I don't go there often. I don't like seeing the
others, the sick. They're all decrepit. And unshaven. I
avoid talking to them. What would we talk about anyway?

There was nobody there except two old men bent over
a wireless set that was blaring out military marches inter-
spersed with short items of news. I asked them to turn
down the volume. They refused. I stood up and switched
off the wireless myself. They didn't even react.

By the time I got back up to my room, I was in a bad mood.

Thursday 27 July 1939

They took Sapperstein away this morning. The gauleiter is *cleaning up* the city for the festival, before the distinguished guests arrive. They came into the canteen at breakfast time and whispered a few words in his ear, politely. Sapperstein stood up and limped out after them, without saying goodbye to anyone. I wonder who could have tipped them off. I must remain on my guard.

Nobody here suspects my ancestry. All the same, I went to the town hall just before noon, to be on the safe side. My birth certificate doesn't mention my father's religion. But there is my sister Gertrude and her Jewish husband. I've no idea what's become of them. They left all of a sudden, without warning. For America, I think.

Monday 31 July 1939

The custodian's son has brought back my suit from the dry cleaner's and I've polished my best shoes. It's all very exciting. I strut in front of the mirror. I've bought a cream to look less pale. It makes me seem oddly younger. And a ribbon for my typewriter.

I'm feeling fine. I drink lots of tea.

Tuesday 1 August 1939

At lunchtime, the grand opening of the festival was announced over the radio. Minister Goebbels has come specially. Hans hasn't been able to get me a ticket for the gala evening. I opened the window of the dayroom to hear the fanfares, the sirens of the official motorcade, the cars hooting their horns in the distance. It was like another world. But a nurse came running, closed the window, and told me off. Is she afraid our germs will escape and contaminate the Great Reich? Then I saw the two old men from the other day, sniggering. So this was how they'd got their revenge, by complaining to the staff. One of them shook so much with laughter that he started coughing very loudly, almost choking. He couldn't breathe. Well done! He was the one who'd asked for the window to remain shut.

I didn't go down for the evening meal. I had no wish to see the other patients all shriveled up in their pajamas or dressing gowns. I donned full evening dress, with a silk handkerchief in my breast pocket, if you please. I put *Der Rosenkavalier* on the phonograph and closed my eyes, imagining the auditorium, the uniforms, the men in tails, the women in their furs and their jewelry, the orchestra tuning up. I even held my pencil between my fingers and pretended I was smoking a cigar. And then I fell into a very deep sleep. Now, it's three o'clock in the morning. The silence scares me. I don't want to die. Not in the middle of the *Festspiele*.

I think about Maria, about mother and father, and about all those who are gone, who died before all this started. What about my son? He's stopped writing. If he sends me a letter from Palestine, I'll be questioned, perhaps even arrested. I have nobody left. I live surrounded by dying men, bad-tempered nurses, dashing soldiers, busy civilians, alone, in the wings. I'm not on stage anymore. Everything is gradually disappearing. And will never return.

Monday 14 August 1939

I've just come back from the concert, exhausted. I can hardly breathe, but I wouldn't have missed it for the world. *Die Entführung aus dem Serail*, conducted by Karl Böhm, in a production by Völker. Kautsky and Ulrich Roller also took part in the venture, which will go down in history. What style! Mozart has never been performed like that before. It was brilliant. Powerful. Astonishing!

Adolf Hitler was there. With Bormann and Speer. In the royal box. I had to crane my neck to see them. He isn't very tall. He was half hidden by the rail. There were guards everywhere. Soldiers in full dress uniform around the auditorium and on the stairs, and hundreds more soldiers in battledress outside. Men in plain clothes checking the invitations. Police officers in the cloakroom, in the foyer bar, outside the toilets. You get used to them always being in the background. There are so many of them. Mostly young. They stand very straight, without saying a word, without disturbing anyone. Plunged into darkness along with the rest of us as soon as the curtain rises.

When the performance starts, the presence of the Führer is palpable. It hovers over the auditorium. But before long, the sumptuousness of the sets, the intensity of the sound, the genius of the music, carry everyone away. Into a sublime region. I took notes discreetly, with my notebook on my lap. Usually, I can detect the slightest wrong note. The smallest scraping of bow on string jars on my eardrums. Tonight, everything sounded perfect. Was it because I'm sick?

At the intermission, I found I was unable to stand. My handwriting is shaky. The seats next to me were empty. Nobody I could ask for a glass of water. I thought the performance would never start again. Music keeps me going. It's the only thing I have left.

Hitler didn't reappear until the lights had gone down again, preceded by his bodyguards. I looked up at his box, and started to wonder. A clash of cymbals made me jump. I was reminded of Stendhal: "a pistol shot in the middle of a concert." I don't have a pistol.

Very tired. This evening was much too stimulating for a sick man. A cold shower of sound and color that makes your head spin. I envy those who can breathe deeply, who can walk without difficulty. The world belongs to them. All they have to do is hold out their hands. Parades, public holidays, military balls, walks in the forest. All these things are forbidden me now. Yet I was like them once. When I was in good health, *normal*. And then, all at once, I was proscribed, marked. By disease. From one day to the next. Contaminated. Not good for very much anymore. Useless.

Hitler's right. People like me are dead weights, parasites.

*

People like me.

Friday 18 August 1939
Fillet of cod, boiled potatoes. I had two spoonfuls. God, how bland it is. I remembered Sapperstein, who wouldn't touch pork.

*

Hans didn't publish my article, claiming a lack of space.

He was expecting me to find fault with the excess of Teutonic grandiloquence. It's true there was a kind of Wagnerian exaggeration in the interpretation. Too dramatic. Mozart is more subtle than that. More fluid. I got carried away by the percussion, the vigorous sounds of the horn and the oboes, Böhm's fiery conducting. And even the braggadocio of the flags and the uniforms. Like everyone.

I could have made a passing reference to Austrian reserve and good taste, the little nods that Mozart makes to the informed spectator in between the big effects intended for the general public. But the whole of the press is calling it a masterpiece, praising the glory of *our* culture, cheering our music-loving soldiers. So why should I stand out for my acerbic comments? That kind of criticism is unfashionable these days. And it's risky.

*

The chest pains have started up again. I can't get to sleep. The first rays of the sun burn my eyes. I ought to close the shutters. No, that would be even more confining.

The pain is becoming less specific. It's spreading like water in the hold of a ship. It makes my limbs go numb. I have less and less strength to resist the currents.

Thursday 24 August 1939

I was very surprised that the Party should authorize a production of *Le Bourgeois Gentilhomme* by Strauss and Hofmannsthal. Because of the subject. And also because of the dubious nature of this new staging. I had the privilege to attend the very first performance in Vienna, some twenty years ago, superbly conducted by Richard Strauss himself. How can one compare such an artistic event with the awful pastiche I had to suffer through at the Stadttheater yesterday?

Heinz Hilpert doesn't even look like a conductor. He holds himself like a drill sergeant, too close to the rostrum. He seems to be haranguing the musicians, as if trying to shake them up instead of leading them. He over-emphasizes the baroque sonorities during the minuets, slaughtering Lully, and when he really ought to show a strong grip, in the ballets or the duels, he slackens off.

I almost left before the end, and not because I was tired. But I go out all too rarely to cut short one of the few evenings when I can mingle with the crowd, stroll about the circles without anyone wanting to put me to bed or give me an injection. Few people understand the delights of being *like everyone else*. For a pariah like me, it's intoxicating. The pleasure of passing unobserved, of melting into the anonymous mass of those who have the right to carry on living. Of letting oneself be carried along with the flow. It's as if one were suddenly accepted. Without displaying one's condition. Without a sign on one's chest saying: PATIENT.

But *Le Bourgeois Gentilhomme*? What an unfortunate choice. Dangerous, even. Isn't that strutting lout with his aristocratic pretensions, that self-important Monsieur Jourdain who shouts and screams to sound like an orator, just a bit like Hitler?

I hadn't seen an audience laugh so heartily for a very long time. Nobody seemed to be making the connection, even though it was staring them in the face. Even the grimaces, the emphatic gestures. The bursts of temper.

But there's nothing amusing about Monsieur Jourdain. Hasn't he finally gained the upper hand over those who made fun of him? It's his caste that's leading the world now. For a thousand years! In any case, I didn't have any desire to laugh. Laughing leaves me breathless.

So I didn't write anything flattering about the performance. A colleague of mine came out with quite a different analysis. He compared that grotesque bourgeois with a Jewish capitalist. According to him, Molière chose the name of the unsavory fellow specifically to condemn those yokels from the banks of the Jordan who want to monopolize everything with their money and think they can hide their hideous appearance beneath their frock coats and top hats and silk ties. They get in everywhere. Even the army, like Dreyfus. But they don't fool anyone. Especially not Mozart, he concluded.

Saturday 26 August 1939

Dr. Müller is very angry with me. He says my excursions are endangering my health and especially the health of the others. Yesterday, he ordered a chest X-ray. My lungs are swarming with germs. He showed me the patches on the negative. It's very contagious. He threatens me with an ablation if I don't behave myself. He treats me like a naughty child.

I thank my father every day for not having me circumcised. Dr. Müller is a great admirer of National Socialism. He examines me once a week, from top to bottom. Was he the one who informed on Sapperstein? To avoid trouble?

*

What if I had coughed at the concert, beneath the royal box, spreading my germs everywhere . . .

Monday 28 August 1939
The *Festspiele* has been cut short. There was a brief, rather curt announcement on the wireless. A whole week has been cancelled. The closing concert, scheduled for 8 September, won't now take place, apparently because the Vienna Philharmonic has to travel to Nuremberg to perform *Die Meistersinger* at the Party Congress. It's scandalous. Appalling!

*

Signed a standing order so that I don't have to keep going to the bank. The treasurer of the sanitarium has given me a discount. If I die, the sanitarium's management committee will be my executor. It will take care of the formalities. And pocket all the money. Dieter is hardly going to come back from Palestine and raise an objection. I said he was in America, pursuing his studies. In Maine. The treasurer didn't even ask me for his address. In any case, there's not much left in my account. And the rent I get for my small apartment just about covers the cost of my board and lodging. The rest goes on the treatment. My tenants are a nice young couple. He's a train driver, I think. His wife works from home as a seamstress. They've never come to see me. Well, as long as they pay their rent on time . . .

It's all a question of what holds out longer, my lungs or my wallet.

*

Thursday 31 August 1939

A patient showed me a newspaper article about bacterial infections. Apparently, a German scientist has discovered a treatment that can cure some kinds of tuberculosis. Dr. Müller says it's too soon to talk about it. The discovery is a recent one, and needs to be tested. The pharmaceutical companies are overwhelmed with commissions from the government for other products that are more urgent. And that also need testing.

In any case, the development of this new medicine may well be delayed because of something that strikes me as absurd. Something that has nothing to do with medical matters. The scientist in question, Gerhard Domagk, is in serious trouble with the authorities because he's been awarded the Nobel Prize this year. For this particular discovery, as it happens. Even though it's strictly forbidden for any German citizen to accept the prize since the Swedes have given it to opponents of the National Socialist regime. And to Jews. That's the way they decide things now.

Friday 1 September 1939

This morning, the armies of the Reich invaded Poland. A surprise attack. Now it's clear why the gauleiter cut short the *Festspiele* by a week.

I remember *my* war. Especially the noise. The cannon fire, the yelling of the officers, the neighing of the horses. And the menacing silence at night, just before dawn. But that was something else, the *Great War*. It lasted four years!

*

I've just come back from the canteen. The others irritate me. They're all worked up. They talk about troop movements, and panzers. They pass the newspaper around. There's a map of the combat zone on the front page. They're delighted. As if this offensive had anything at all to do with us. Who cares about Poland?

*

I didn't even glance at the daily paper. I prefer the news in brief on the wireless. One sentence per subject, short and sharp. *This morning, the German armies invaded Poland.* That's all you need. I should write my memoirs in the same concise, telegraphic style. *Didn't go down to the canteen this evening. Reread beginning of* Werther.

The silence of my room comforts me for once. After all the commotion. I'm really pleased that I'm no longer part of all that.

Sunday 3 September 1939
Bad day. Coughing like an old man. Unable to stop. The tea burns my throat. When it's cold, it makes me nauseous.

There may be a war on, but the city has never seemed so peaceful. Through the window, I can hear the sparrows chirping in the trees out in the courtyard. As it's Sunday, there's a reduced staff. Everyone's resting. Even the wireless is off.

I'm coming down with something, I'm sure of it. Tonsillitis, perhaps. I don't dare bother the duty nurse. Everything is so calm. The disease is running its course. Inexorably. What's the point of calling for help?

Friday 22 September 1939
Three weeks in bed, with fever and stomach pains. I look at myself in the mirror. In hospital pajamas, dirty and creased. My face emaciated, yellowish. I've lost several pounds. I can barely stand on my feet. I'm starting to look like the patients on the third floor, the advanced stage. We never see them. Or very rarely. We can hardly hear them. Everyone prefers to avoid the third floor. Even those of us who are already seriously ill. Out of superstition, I suppose.

Apart from the nurses and the cleaning woman, I haven't seen anybody. The doctor only came once. He told me it wasn't serious. I just have to drink a lot until it passes. I didn't even ask him how the war was going. Maybe it's already over.

Monday 25 September 1939
Freud died the day before yesterday. Euthanasia. He had cancer of the mouth. All those cigars . . . Three doses of morphine and it was all over. It's food for thought. He left Austria *in extremis*, in 1938. That was something I thought about too.

Thursday 5 October 1939
Autumn is good for me.
I went down at teatime to listen to the radio. Everyone

was there. All present and correct. Too bad. There's a new arrival. As consumptive as could be. He coughs a lot, covering his hand with his mouth in embarrassment. He's not used to it yet.

I remember my first day. The disease was one thing. But finding myself there, suddenly, among these dying men . . . At the beginning, I looked at them like a spectator, as if from a distance. Even now, I avoid their eyes. And anyway, I've learned to stop paying attention to them. Especially those who moan and groan. I've learned to obey the house rules. Or at least to give that impression. To always be polite to Dr. Müller. To obey the nurses, even though their dictatorial manner is so off-putting. To bribe the custodian's son with candies. I've gotten into the habit without anybody telling me. Without anybody having to explain. Instinctively.

The newcomer sits in his corner, away from everyone else. Nobody talks to him. He seems embarrassed to be here. And shy. He doesn't dare look up at us, the veterans. He'll learn eventually. Or not.

*

I've just heard planes in the sky. They passed very close, just above the upper town. For the first time, I feel something. That there's a war. That I'm stuck here with the others. Difficult to get back to sleep.

Friday 6 October 1939
Cod and boiled potatoes. I'll never get used to it.

Sunday 8 October 1939

Listened to Chopin on my phonograph, then went down to the courtyard for a walk. The newcomer was there, sitting on a bench. He told me he was very fond of Chopin. He didn't introduce himself. I didn't reply.

*

The nights are more and more interminable. I'm too tired to read. In any case, I'm soon going to be forced to sell off my books if I want the custodian's son to keep buying me saveloy. I'll start by selling the libretti, because I know them all by heart. The Italian operas first. Mozart last.

*

I had a dream I founded an orchestra. With the patients. It was quite amusing. All those skeletons in their pajamas playing Schubert at the door of the canteen! Too comical for words.

Thought again about my mother and her viola. The hours of practice in the drawing room, going over and over the same piece. At the time it used to get on my nerves. What a perfectionist! I attended dozens of her concerts at the Mozarteum. She wouldn't look for me in the auditorium, she kept her eyes on her score. And as a critic myself, I avoided listening too closely to the strings. She was stiff, too wedded to the notes. Very provincial. Not at all Viennese. I think about her more and more. Which surprises me.

Wednesday 18 October 1939
My phonograph isn't working very well. The crank mechanism is worn. It's too expensive to replace it. The records are there, lined up on the lower shelf. I take out an album at random and hum the tune from memory. With variations. Eyes closed.

*

I saw a gurney pass at the end of the corridor. Covered in a sheet. Usually I don't take any notice. It's not like at the beginning. But this corpse was taken away in a magnificent hearse, without going through the morgue. A funeral cortege.

*

Downstairs, in the canteen, five or six patients were missing. Impossible to know who was just poorly and who had gone to the funeral. Strangely, I remembered that the Jews require at least ten men to recite the prayer for the dead. Where could I have heard that? What happens if there aren't ten men?

Monday 23 October 1939
Yesterday, a gloomy Sunday.

Saturday 28 October 1939
I thought I was hallucinating, off my head. With all these wretched drugs. I actually suspect Müller of using us as guinea pigs. Anyway, I heard some Chopin. In the dis-

tance. The E major Scherzo. The notes of the piano hovered over the courtyard, slid between the foliage of the plane trees, bounced cheerfully off the wall of the covered yard. So there's someone else who has a phonograph. It must be the new patient. I'll find out on Monday, from the cleaning woman.

*

On reflection, it doesn't really matter where the music came from or who has a phonograph. I've resigned myself to the idea that mine is broken, and I get along perfectly well without it.

Thursday 9 November 1939
Assassination attempt on Hitler in Munich yesterday. By a Communist. With a bomb. But the Führer wasn't there. He had left earlier than planned to catch the train, the bad weather having prevented him from getting back to Berlin by plane. Several people were killed. It was a close-run thing.

*

Three o'clock in the morning. Insomnia. It's raining. It's true the weather is bad.

*

Five o'clock. Still dark. Is it so easy, then? To kill him?

Saturday 18 November 1939

Al Capone was released from jail on Thursday. I imagined him leaving his prison uniform in the cloakroom and emerging from the gate of the penitentiary in an impeccable suit, a cigar in his mouth, in beautiful winter sunshine. As if he were leaving a business meeting.

I looked at my good clothes in the wardrobe. I considered going out. It's nice outside. It's one of the last decent days. Before the cold really sets in.

*

I would have done better to go out. I slipped a couple of banknotes to the cleaning woman. To let me feel her up. I looked like an idiot, with my hands on her breasts. She was kind. She rubbed me a little. Nothing happened. Even though I wanted it . . . Nothing.

*

I feel colder and colder.

Tuesday 21 November 1939

Hans came to see me. He talked a lot about the war. Several young musicians have left for the front. He's managed to get himself declared unfit for service. He was wearing a gas mask, in order not to catch my germs. He brought me some cookies. I didn't have much to say to him. We talked about Karajan, his meteoric rise, his career, his concerts in Berlin. I'm a bit jealous. I told Hans that Karajan was too heavy-handed, that he had talent but wasted it in trying to appeal to the masses. Hans didn't like that. I don't know if he'll be back in a hurry. But I had to say something, to make it seem as though I'm up to date. To fill in the gaps.

*

On reflection, I'm sorry I behaved so boorishly toward Hans. None of this is his fault, the war, the tuberculosis, Karajan's fame. He was quite brave to come here, to the sanitarium. It can't be very entertaining. But how to make him understand? The degradation, the constant proximity of death. That hospital smell, which I'm sure repels him, I don't even smell anymore. I'm part of it, and it's part of me. It stinks like the cod on Friday. How to tell Hans that it isn't the bacteria that cause this decay? It's the drab corridors, the grey walls around the courtyard, the languor that envelops everything like a shroud.

Monday 4 December 1939
Total hibernation. The window panes are covered in frost. The radiator is working badly. It hisses. I went down to the canteen for the first time in about two weeks. The newcomer gave me a little smile. He's lost a lot of weight.

The wireless talks about the Russians, the Italians, the British. Everything has become huge. Millions of men, hundreds of bombs, billions of Deutschmarks. It's all meaningless.

Received a letter from my tenant. Her husband has been enlisted. The trains he drives now are going east. She has no money left to pay the rent. I threw the letter in the trash. The treasurer told me he would contact the railway administrators to make sure I'm compensated. I didn't believe him.

There's nobody to count on but oneself. It's pointless expecting anything from other people.

Wednesday 6 December 1939

Some detectives came and searched our rooms. And the library. They were looking for decadent works. At first I thought they meant the Romantics. But no, they didn't touch my nineteenth-century editions. My opera librettos in Italian didn't seem to interest them either. The French books rather more. I told them that Anatole France was a professor at the Conservatory. My collection is mostly devoted to music. They quickly shuffled a few of my records and then left. *Heil Hitler!*

It was the first time anyone had given me the official salute, with the arm well extended. I've trained myself to do it, in front of the mirror.

Dr. Müller came to examine me, even though it isn't my day. I think he was surprised the policemen hadn't found anything compromising in my room. I almost gave him the Nazi salute, to force him to reciprocate.

Friday 15 December 1939

Boiled potatoes, but no cod. Rationing. The custodian's son says you can still find saveloy on the black market. Too expensive.

There's a Christmas tree in the canteen. It hasn't been decorated yet. I'd really like to meet Father Christmas this year. I'd give him a piece of my mind.

The wireless crackles, because of the snow. The reception is bad. As if that weren't enough, most of the patients have caught cold, and they cough and sneeze in unison just when the news is coming on. The Russians are marching on Finland. The snow doesn't bother them.

Wednesday 20 December 1939
I haven't seen the newcomer for several days. Neither in the canteen nor in the dayroom. I was told he's not well at all. That they're thinking to transfer him to the third floor. The third floor is to be avoided at all costs.

*

For the first time, I thought about suicide. About ending it all. I wondered how to go about it. Get drunk and then throw myself naked in a river. Or out the window. But the rivers are frozen at this time of year, and the building isn't high enough, with all this snow. Maybe I should wait until spring.

Sunday 24 December 1939
Christmas Eve. Pope Pius XII calls for peace. *Pax.* The tree has been decorated. Below it, someone has placed a little crèche filled with papier-mâché figures. Decent meal, given the circumstances. Unusually lively atmosphere in the canteen. I waited as long as possible to go back up to my room.

Monday 25 December 1939
Christmas.

Thursday 4 January 1940
My tenant is penniless. Her husband isn't sending her
any money. He's somewhere in Poland, or Yugoslavia, I
can't remember which.

To make my savings last, I've resigned myself to aban-
doning my private quarters. I'm going to be transferred to
Ward 5, which has six beds. And a view of the courtyard.

A record dealer came to buy my phonograph, which
has stopped working, and my collection. He took advantage of my situation, the bastard. I know the exact value of
each record, each score. He offered me less than a tenth.
Take it or leave it. Business is bad, he says. Because of the
war. Life is hard. He dared say that to me, *life is hard . . .*
The room looks empty now. I'm ashamed of myself. For
selling my music cheap. War or no war. And for going to
the Nazis' *Festspiele.* It's unforgivable. How can I redeem
myself?

Saturday 6 January 1940
I don't dare look at myself in the mirror. I'm convinced,
though, that I must look better than the others. It's just that
I've lost a lot of weight since the custodian's son stopped
bringing me saveloy. My clothes hang loose on me.

The trees in the courtyard are bare. Their leafless
branches sway in the wind, as if they too were shivering
with cold.

Sunday 7 January 1940

Hans paid me a surprise visit. I suspect the management of informing him of my financial situation. He offered me money. A loan. I refused. But I did accept the nice box of cookies he brought. Viennese macaroons. What a delight!

He says the news is quite good. The Reich is winning on all fronts. He also says that times are hard. Just like the record dealer. The Jews have been transferred. And the gypsies. They're contributing to the war effort. Like everyone else. Even Karajan is giving free concerts for the soldiers. And Hans is already preparing the program for the next festival, this summer.

Hans promised to come back and see me again next month. He's going skiing. I didn't tell him I'm being moved to a general ward.

*

I hope my sister is in America. I can't exactly see her contributing to the war effort. Her manicured nails, her well-groomed hair, her aristocratic airs . . .

Monday 8 January 1940

Impossible to sleep. I think about my sister, my nephews, and even my brother-in-law, who I don't like, with his spectacles perched on the end of his nose. Oh, these doctors . . . I'm worried about them. I have a bad feeling. Of course, I can't do anything for them. Especially in my condition. I'd just like to know. What's the connection between the Jews and the Gypsies? They have nothing in common. Apart perhaps from being wanderers.

I really can't get to sleep.

*

I may not need to kill myself. There's been much talk of euthanasia lately.

Friday 12 January 1940
My birthday. Boiled potatoes. No cod. But I did get a nice present from Dr. Müller. An extra week in a private room, at the sanitarium's expense. Müller's not such a bad sort after all. He knows how hard it's going to be for me to live in a general ward. I can't bear the other patients, their smells, their slow gestures, their negligent attire.

I again considered going out, even if it means dropping dead two streets from here. For my birthday. It's a good day to make resolutions. So I set myself a goal. Go one last time to the *Festspiele*, in suit and tie. It's in about six months. If I can only hold out until then, even in a shared ward, even surrounded by the stench of disease.

I don't think I'm likely to get better. Just delay the end. The symptoms are there, clear for all to see. The unmistakable signs that my illness is running its course. I'm not pretending to ignore them. I'm not burying my head in the sand. It's just that one should never envisage the worst.

Sunday 14 January 1940
The newcomer died last night. On the second floor! That's never happened before. The incurables are kept on

the third floor. And those who can't pay for their continued treatment.

I thought about him. All stiff in a drawer in the morgue. It's funny, I wasn't sad. Just irritated. As if annoyed with him for dying on our floor and not on the third. I don't even know his name. I rejected his company, his advances. As soon as he arrived, I could see he wasn't going to pull through. So what would have been the point?

*

Decided to do a little investigating. One of the nurses has family in Vienna. I didn't tell her about my sister, obviously. Only about the building, telling her I had friends there that I wanted to write to, the Haüsers, but I wasn't sure of the exact address, if it was 45 or 47, or maybe even 46 opposite. The Haüsers are neighbors and friends of my brother-in-law. They live on the fourth floor. And my sister on the third.

Monday 15 January 1940
I should never have asked that service of the nurse. I really regret it now. It's gotten me worried. I'm going to tell her I changed my mind, that there's no point.

Or is it better to say nothing?

*

What's the point of keeping this damn diary? I must get rid of it.

*

Wednesday 17 January 1940
This morning, the custodian's son came and knocked at my door. The boiler has been under repair since the day before yesterday. He found my notebook as he was cleaning. I looked like a fool. He gave it back to me with a sardonic grin. How does he know the diary is mine? Has he read it?

If I try to get rid of it again, it'll look suspicious. So why continue? To what purpose? I could write lies in it, to cover myself, to avert suspicion. What am I scared of anyway? I probably won't last the winter, Hitler or no Hitler. Am I writing for Dieter? To make him feel guilty? My beloved son doesn't care what happens to me. He left to change the world. A long way from here. To make sure his past doesn't catch up with him. His bourgeois past. I can't blame him. My past is certainly catching up with me, after all this time. My Jewish past. All because of a stupid diary. And an out-of-order boiler.

Thursday 18 January 1940
As Dr. Müller was conducting his examination, he reminded me that I'm moving to Ward 5 next Monday. I have the weekend to get myself organized before I leave my room. He ran through the house rules as they applied to wards of six beds, and then, in a confidential tone, advised me to be more careful in future. Not to leave my things lying around!

I promised him I wouldn't write anything more. I don't know why that made him laugh. He just repeated that I shouldn't leave my things lying around just anywhere. Or trust the nurses. And then he gave me the information I wanted, in that grave, neutral doctor's manner of his. My sister doesn't live in Vienna anymore. And she didn't leave for America. The doctor told me that, when it came to Sapperstein, he had no choice. He informed on him to be straight with the authorities. So that the sanitarium would be left in peace. It was the price he had to pay. But it's still necessary to exercise caution.

I don't know if I should be grateful to him.

*

This diary has definitely brought me an unwanted fame. Because of it, I've stupidly drawn attention to myself. They know. And now they're waiting.

Saturday 20 January 1940

The newcomer's niece has donated her late uncle's phonograph and records to the sanitarium. The doctor has put them in the canteen so that we can eat to music. To cover the noise of coughing, the scraping of knives and forks on the plates.

I find it grim. Beethoven in the canteen of a sanitarium, with all these invalids in their dressing gowns. Not to mention the fact that the acoustics are terrible, because of the cement walls and the tiles. I told the manager. He replied that it was the dead man's wish. But what about the living?

I never thought I would ever come to loathe Beethoven.

*

But why was the newcomer so eager for us to listen to his old records? By forcing everyone to remember him, he's made himself completely detestable. Many others have gone before him, without saying anything, without leaving any trace. Without boasting!

Was it to remind us that it's also possible to die on the second floor?

*

I should have asked him his name. The better to forget it.

Sunday 21 January 1940
I've packed my bags. It's my last day in a private room. I take advantage of every remaining moment. The silence, the solitude, alone in my shell. Who would ever have thought it's possible to miss solitude? Some soldiers are passing outside. In rhythm. Beating the sidewalk.

Monday 22 January 1940
Moved to Ward 5. Hard to take.

I've had to wait for the others to get to sleep before I could write. They were polite enough, though. They didn't bombard me with questions. One of them simply asked me if I played chess. He looks quite distinguished, in spite of his rumpled pajamas. On his bedside table, I noticed a family photograph taken in the doorway of a large building.

I made a big effort not to seem too grumpy. I don't know what to do to get rid of the bad smells. I have no more cologne.

Let's hope Hans doesn't pay me any more visits. Not here.

Tuesday 23 January 1940

This diary irritates me. It throws me back a distorted image of myself, like the cracked mirror in the corridor. An image that's increasingly similar to everyone else, the patients in Ward 5, or in the canteen, with their empty eyes and fixed grins like characters from a cheap horror film. As if they had all come to an agreement to pull the same faces. No! It's not me I see in their vampire eyes, in the cracked mirror, in this dog-eared exercise book. I truly don't recognize myself in these clipped, staccato sentences, even though I wrote them with my own hand. I reread them sometimes as if they were the memoirs of a stranger. Or of a ghost.

I'm going to have to fight all these lies.

Thursday 25 January 1940

A patient from our ward has been transferred to the third floor. His bed sits there empty, like a threat, a verdict.

*

My neighbor in the ward had visitors. He received them downstairs in the entrance hall. An elegant woman and two adolescents dressed in their Sunday best. They wept a lot. In chorus. And then he came back up. I told him I

could play chess. We had a game. Without saying any-
thing. His mind was elsewhere. I won. He shook my hand.
He has a firm grip. Firmer than mine. His name is Günter.
Günter Ratenau.

*

Went down to listen to the wireless. Our submarines
have sunk several cargo ships, French, Norwegian, British.
The Jews are no longer allowed to travel by train. The
Russians are still fighting the Finns. Tomorrow, there will
be snow in Salzburg and over most of the country.

Monday 29 January 1940
Confined to bed since yesterday. The night watchman
found me in the courtyard. Frozen stiff.
Saturday was very hard. As soon as I woke, I could feel
that things weren't good. Dry throat, shivering, chest
pains, back pains, cramps, nausea. I didn't want to say anything. From beneath the sheets, I saw the others as if in a
fog. Like puppets in a shadow play. I couldn't breathe, as
if I was drowning. Günter brought me some water. Water
for a drowning man?
At night, it was even worse. High temperature, diar-
rhea. Shame. Anger. When the others at last fell asleep, I
dragged myself to the courtyard and lay down in the snow.
I looked at the branches of the trees, the sky, a beam of
moonlight.
That suicide did me good.

Friday 2 February 1940
The cod is back. The potatoes, boiled with them, smell of fish. And of hospital stench. Impossible to cut. Just watching the others swallow makes me want to throw up. Which is what I did. In front of everybody.

*

When Dieter was little . . . Five or six . . . In the park. The balloons. The band. Maria.

*

All this is because of Hitler.

Saturday 3 February 1940
Saturday, the Sabbath. What made me think of that?

*

My chest hurts. As if it were shrinking. Tuberculosis can take on different forms, diffuse, meningeal, pulmonary, depending on where the seat of infection is located. It can spread throughout the body if it isn't treated in time. It has to be neutralized from the start, before it's too late.

*

Game of chess with Günter. He won. But with no style. He grouped all his pawns on the right-hand side of the board, forcing me to play defensively in order to block him. I should have sent my bishop off to the left and created a diversion. His king wasn't well protected. I should have looked for his weak spot.

Sunday 4 February 1940
Too tired to play.

Wednesday 7 February 1940
Health inspection. They spent ages on the third floor. Dr. Müller was uneasy. The rest of the staff too. From my bed, I glimpsed two men passing in the corridor, looking pressed for time, their noses in lists. They weren't wearing white coats. One of them had a limp. His wooden leg knocked on the tiled floor. Luckily they didn't come into Ward 5. Nobody's even cleaned the ward for three days.

*

I'm finding it hard to get as far as the wash basin. I thought about the drugs locked in the medicine cabinet. Morphine? Curare? In the absence of a good cognac.

Thursday 8 February 1940
My tenant came! She brought me a steaming bacon hotpot in lieu of rent. She apologized for her delay in paying, but promises to let me have *a little something* next month. Her husband will be getting a bonus. Austrian Railways has reached an agreement whereby it will be

remunerated at the official rate for trains commissioned by the army. Particularly the special eastbound trains. A separate fund has been allocated for the production of new engines that will increase efficiency and allow the workers and their machines to rest a little between journeys. Her husband is exhausted. When he comes home for a day or two, he collapses on the bed and falls fast asleep. He doesn't talk to her. Either about the war or about the weather. Or even about his work.

She's young and fresh-looking, with her blonde braids and pink cheeks. Like a little girl. The others were jealous.

Günter told me I was lucky to have such honest tenants. There's no lack of empty apartments that used to belong to Jews. Or communists. They're often the same, he said with a laugh. I thought about my brother-in-law. A bourgeois and a snob. And my father who so wanted to be a Christian.

*

I dreamed about those train journeys, like a little boy. The cars gliding over the rails, cutting through the misty countryside, whistling in the darkness, taking you to the ends of the earth.

Friday 9 February 1940
Boiled potatoes? Forget it! I gave my *Werther* to the custodian's son. With the money he got for it he bought me a piece of saveloy on the black market. Delicious!

Saturday 10 and Sunday 11 February 1940
Praying is out of the question. Absolutely! Why did I think about God? It's against my principles. There's a little chapel at the far end of the covered yard. Pews, unlit candles, a painted wooden crucifix. I only went to have a look.

*

I refused to play chess with Günter. He gets on my nerves with his comments on current events, the latest from the front, the Führer's speeches. Nothing to make a fuss about. History's taking its course, that's all.

They run tests on me every week. What's happening to me is staring me in the face. The infection is spreading. No need to be a doctor to know that! Just sick.

Tuesday 13 February 1940
Checkmate in sixteen moves! I sacrificed all my soldiers and then charged in, heading straight for the king. Günter was taken by surprise. He collapsed on his bed, exhausted.

I went out into the courtyard, in spite of the cold. A nurse told me off. I sent her packing. I even swore at her. She ran away.

*

When Dr. Müller examined me he told me I was looking well. I found myself staring at the medicine cabinet, just behind him. He smiled. Don't even think about it, my dear fellow. *But yes, I am thinking about it.*

*

Thursday 15 February 1940

A strange visit from Hans, who sprained his ankle skiing. He was depressed, having his leg in plaster just when he has to get down to the preparations for the summer festival. I was the one who had to cheer him up.

He showed me a score by a young composer. I liked it a lot. Lively and optimistic. Hans doesn't share my opinion, but the cultural committee is forcing him to include it in the program for the next *Festspiele*. As with the whole program, in fact. Most of the audience will be military: officers, war heroes, the seriously wounded. Just one orchestra, the Vienna Philharmonic. Böhm, Furtwängler and Lehár will conduct. Not Karajan. Decisions taken at a high level. Not very encouraging, to be honest. All the concerts will be broadcast on the wireless. For a few evenings Salzburg will be the capital of the Reich, and of music.

Very flattered that Hans asked me to help him by writing the program notes. And even the introduction to the official brochure. And then I realized. Hans is scared. Every sentence will be gone over by the Party's cultural committee. The smallest slip could get him into trouble. But I have nothing to lose.

I promised to help him. I owe him that at least. After all, he's the only one who still comes to see me. Apart from my tenant. The others have severed relations with me rather too quickly for my taste. In their place, I would probably have done the same.

By the time Hans left, limping on his crutches, I seemed to have set his mind at rest. He left me a box of macaroons. I thought I might give it to my tenant, if she comes back.

*

I can understand how helpless Hans must feel. The Nazis' meddling in the program for the *Festspiele* is intolerable. Revolting. Turning the Festival into a mere propaganda tool, an entertainment for the troops, is the last straw. Taking Mozart hostage. Demeaning him in that way. Isn't there anyone who can prevent such an outrage?

This time they've gone too far! They can't be allowed to do such a thing. There has to be some way to react. This farce must be stopped. At all costs. Mozart must be saved!

Saturday 17 February 1940
Saint Günter. He won my box of macaroons at chess and then went and shared them among the patients on the third floor. That's how I learned that he takes care of them. Whenever he disappears, it's to go upstairs. I hadn't even noticed. He spends hours there. What does he do with them in all that time? Is he their nurse, their confessor?

He told me about an old man, who's in a very bad way, can't remember anything and raves most of the time, but is unbeatable at chess. He doesn't even recognize Günter although he comes to see him every day. He never gets out of his bed. During the game, he hardly looks at the board, just stares up at the ceiling with his glassy eyes. Only from time to time, when Günter shakes him, he'll give a brief glance at the board and then dictate his move: rook to G5. He can no longer move the pieces. He gets checkmate in twelve moves, not one more, not one less, whatever happens.

I'm surprised Dr. Müller lets Günter move about like

that on the third floor. It's against the rules. Fortunately, the patients upstairs are not allowed to come down, as a hygienic measure. Nothing's very logical in this hospital. Why put the dying all the way upstairs, as far as possible from the exit?

Tuesday 20 February 1940
Two visitors!

The first was Hans. He suddenly showed up in the ward just before the time for washing. I was in my pajamas, and unshaven. He brought me the literature I need to start work. He advised me to follow the news on the wireless, especially the official speeches. To get the tone right. He seemed worried. The gauleiter has asked him to personally choose two or three pieces for the district brass band, in preparation for an event of the greatest importance. That's all he knows. I suggested a few works in which the percussion stand out and the rest of the band doesn't need to be particularly virtuosic, just keep to the beat. He didn't find them solemn enough. Too facile. To be honest, he has no idea what kind of ceremony it'll be. It's a secret. The gauleiter simply gave him to understand that some very important people will be present. Perhaps even the Führer. A simple regimental march won't suffice. Some Wagner, then?

The second visitor was my tenant, who came at lunch time with another bacon hotpot. She paid me half of January's rent. Or was it December's? Her husband will be back soon. He's been recalled to drive a train on the line that goes up to the passes. A new engine is being put to the test. It's a great honor. A mission of trust, was how she put it. His colleagues have congratulated him. He deserves it, after all these months in Poland. She's very proud of him. Her husband isn't a simple railroad man. He drives special trains.

These visits tired me. I couldn't even swallow a spoonful of hotpot. Too heavy. Saint Günter took the saucepan up to the third floor.

What I really want is a cigar.

Thursday 22 February 1940
Very sick since yesterday. Chest X-ray. I wish I could just raid the medicine cabinet.

Sunday 25 February 1940
Not good. Günter waiting on me hand and foot. No strength even to write.

Thursday 29 February 1940
Leap year.

Feeling a little better. I absolutely must start writing for the *Festspiele.* Hans is snowed under with work, not to mention that business of the brass band. And he's scared to death of the SS. So I have to weigh my words, take care not to overdo it, not to insult the works that are going to be played. Mozart still has to be protected from these idiots.

Friday 1 March 1940
My least favorite day of the week. I'm in a bad mood.

Well, at least it sharpens my mind. I may be all skin and bone. But I still have my nerves. And I still have music.

I've never understood music so well as I have since I stopped listening to it. Since I've been forced to do without it. But it has other ways of making itself heard. There's no need for a phonograph. Or a score. The genius of music is the breath that goes through *The Magic Flute* before it emits a single sound. It's the waiting that precedes the hearing. It's the gesture, the attitude, the emotion. Nothing to do with the notes.

I can remember hundreds of melodies, the words of all the great operas, in Italian, German and French, the names of conductors and singers, the applause. It all echoes in my head, throbs in my eardrums. If they take music from me . . .

No, not that! I won't let them.

Saturday 2 March 1940
I'm in the chapel. I can write in peace here.

The figure of Christ sends shivers down my spine. A trickle of blood, too dark in color, runs down his forehead. His crown of thorns is made out of a segment of barbed wire. I avoid looking at him. There's something embarrassing in another person's suffering. Like a reproach. And yet I see suffering people every day. Real people, not wooden figurines. I don't understand.

I can't get the D minor Requiem out of my head. Mozart died before he could finish it. He was about the same age as Jesus.

Monday 4 March 1940

Double dose of tonic pills. They work!

Dr. Müller's medicine cabinet is brimming with treasures. Drugs, poisons, potions. A veritable arsenal of life and death that he can use as and when he wishes. Basically, we're at his mercy. A drop of arsenic here, a dose of morphine there, and it's all over.

To be able to kill whomever one wants, whenever one wants. So many people have that power. Generals, nurses, streetcar drivers who go too fast. There's nothing more commonplace than a homicide. It's within everyone's reach. A motive isn't always necessary. Rather, a state of mind. A desire.

*

The more I write for Hans, the more I realize how preposterous this whole extravaganza is. *Salzburger Kultursommer*, that's the name they've chosen for the *Festspiele* this year. The summer of culture!

Some Beethoven to start, to warm up the audience before hitting it with Bruckner's Seventh. Mahler admired Bruckner's music. He said of him that he was "half-simpleton, half-god." Isn't that how the Germans see Hitler?

For the brochure, I merely mention that the Anton Bruckner Conservatory is in Linz, not far from the house where the Führer was born. Obviously, I don't quote Mahler.

That first concert is reasonable, I suppose. But the second? To have one of Mozart's violin concertos, in the Mozarteum no less, preceded by a composition of Wilhelm Jerger! SS Lieutenant Jerger. Very much in vogue. Like

Karajan. He's in charge of *reorganizing* the Vienna Philharmonic. Which he's gone about doing with the greatest zeal. Hans was personally acquainted with one of the Jewish musicians Jerger has just had deported to the east. A viola player, like my mother. Jerger himself is a bass player. Originally.

From Vienna, Wilhelm Jerger brings us a vigorous modern sound, at once baroque and very pure. That's what I wrote.

Tuesday 5 March 1940

The tonic pills strengthen me. And make me nauseous. Everything disgusts me. I hum passages from *La Traviata*, to forget my heartburn. *Libiamo, ne' lieti calici . . .* Opera was the one and only reason I learned Italian.

I find it hard to work, to concentrate. But I don't want to disappoint Hans. Or abandon Mozart to his grim fate. *O mio rimorso!*

*

Günter is no braver than I am. His elderly chess partner died yesterday morning. It's been a blow to him. He says the only reason he wants to keep going is so that he can carry on taking care of the seriously ill patients on the third floor. Which is not very sensible. Spending all that time with the dying, he risks infecting the rest of us.

I offered him one of my tonic pills. Actually, I'd like to see if they make him nauseous too. I don't trust Dr. Müller.

The atmosphere in the sanitarium disgusts me. I can no longer stand the unremitting presence of those emaciated faces, those cardboard masks all around me, lying in wait for me in the corridors, passing me on the stairs, following me to the latrines. Like shadows.

Saint-Saëns, *Danse macabre*.

Wednesday 6 March 1940

Hans came to see me. Very much on edge. He doesn't look well. He's still limping. His ankle still hasn't healed since the skiing accident.

I had taken refuge in the chapel to write. Who told him where to find me?

He looked through my rough drafts and made a few corrections. He's very pleased with me. I'm a good writer when I want to be. I know how to juggle with grammar, to flush out the perfect word, to turn an elegant sentence. But Hans will still have to submit the texts to the committee, to make sure everything's all right, everything's acceptable.

He brought up the subject of the brass band again. He knows there will be some Italians at the event, some very important Italians. So he needs to dig up a few Italian marches, not just Tyrolean or Bavarian ones. It isn't easy to find any in the library of the Conservatory. Time is short. Only a few days to prepare everything. Hans doesn't know the exact date. Or even the place. But the gauleiter is counting on him. And he's counting on me.

I made fun of Hans and his constant anxieties. He wasn't offended. All he said was: *You don't know how it is out there. What's happening . . .*

And he doesn't know how it is in here.

*

In working as Hans's ghost writer, his slave in a way, I feel as if I'm selling my soul. And betraying Mozart.

We're all slaves of words.

Thursday 7 March 1940

Günter is in a delirious state, and sweating profusely. Last night, for the first time, he spat blood. I took the chessboard out. He dictated a few moves, knight to C4, queen to C5, and then fell asleep. Fortunately for me. He was very close to winning the game.

*

My tenant didn't come. She sent me a pan of soup and a little note to apologize. She's pregnant. Her husband has forbidden her to visit me, because of the germs. With his promotion, they'll have enough to raise the child and pay the rent. The breaking-in stage for the new model of loco-motive is over. It's going to be unveiled in a few days' time, on the line going up to the passes, at an official ceremony. Not only official but secret, she added.

I'm sorry she can't come to see me anymore. I like her. She's gentle, very polite, a little naive. She is the only woman I ever see apart from the nurses. I've even stopped calling on the services of the cleaning woman, who's ugly anyway. I still have the urge to make love. But not like that.

Friday 8 March 1940
Günter's bed is empty. Last night they took him to the third floor. I didn't hear anything.

I miss him. But going upstairs to see him is out of the question. I'll just have to stop thinking about him. Forget him. He's the one who dumped me, after all. Without even finishing our game.

*

Haven't heard from Hans. I hope he isn't in trouble with the Gestapo because of anything I wrote. All I did was slip a few ironic touches in between the lines, a few nods to the more informed spectators. References to the *wise and discriminating choice* of works and the *discipline* of the performances. Anyway, most people who go to concerts don't understand anything about music. They have much too good an ear for that. Dozens of ears, all sitting there in rows, listening. *Transported.*

Strange that the Germans should be such music lovers. Music is a constant process of trial and error . . .

*

The fighting on the Finnish front has intensified. The British government is handing out gas masks to the population. In Warsaw, the Jews have been moved to a specially allocated area. The Reichsbahn has announced the production of a new Meiningen diesel engine, which will be stronger and faster.

Impossible to change the wavelength, the button on the wireless is stuck with glue. The manager told me it was in

order to prevent arguments. One of the patients came up
to me and whispered in my ear that it was to avoid anyone
trying to tune into clandestine radio.

*

I can't forget Günter. I keep trying, but I can't get his
face out of my mind. Like Christ's in the chapel. But more
distinct.

Saturday 9 March 1940
No sign of Hans. I'm worried.
Still nauseous. And finding it harder and harder to
breathe. I'm endlessly clearing my throat, and spitting a
lot, but not blood. Is Doctor Müller poisoning me?
During the examination, he seemed distant, ill at ease. He
didn't say anything when I stared for a long time at the
medicine cabinet. Usually he reprimands me. Don't even
think about it, my dear fellow.
He keeps the key in the pocket of his white coat. At the
end of the day, he leaves the sanitarium in his ordinary suit.
He leaves his coat hanging from a hook on the back of the
door.

Sunday 10 March 1940
Dead calm. Glorious day.
I managed to get into the doctor's office. The key to the
cabinet was there, in his coat. All the flasks are listed, the
levels marked with lines, the doses taken written down in
a little notebook, with the dates. Ditto for the boxes of

pills, with the quantities and dates written on the lids. In a vial, I made up a little mixture for myself with those syrups and liquids that seemed the most harmful. I restored the levels in the flasks with my own urine, up to the marks. There was also a powder, labeled with a skull. I took a few pinches, which I replaced with dust from the floor. Should I swallow the whole thing now and have done with it? It's a lovely day to die.

*

I've decided to go outside one last time and swallow my potion in a park. Or by the river. In short, not to die here like a rat.

Monday 11 March 1940
The wall was too high. And besides, on Sunday the gate is closed and the custodian and his son stay in their lodge and get drunk. Impossible to pass without their seeing me. I'll go out today, just after visiting hours. I'm going to leave this notebook with a notary. Along with my will. In a sealed envelope addressed to Dieter, care of the Austrian Consulate in Haifa. Dieter is an Austrian citizen, after all.

How could I have forgotten to make a will? How can I die without leaving anything?

My dear son,
I'd like you to read this diary as if it were that of a person you've never met.

You are probably the only member of the family still alive. I have no idea what happened to your aunt or your cousins. You were quite right to leave.

Besides the apartment, which I am bequeathing to you, this notebook is all that remains of me. I've written it throughout my illness the better to confront it. Nevertheless, it is this diary, and not my tuberculosis, which has slowly led me toward death. I am dying in it, page by page, inexorably.

Salzburg is very sick too. Infected. I'd set myself the goal of holding out until the next Festspiele. But not anymore. They've turned it into a bazaar for soldiers on leave and louts in evening dress. Music was my last refuge.

At first, I felt ashamed of this sanitarium. All these decrepit bodies, in their hospital pajamas, aimlessly roaming the corridors, gobbling boiled potatoes, or lying motionless on their grubby beds. I didn't want to be like them. Even in my condition.

I wanted to be like the others, the people outside. To go to work or to a restaurant, to keep an amorous rendezvous, to walk on the streets, in the parks. Not anymore. It's the people outside who disgust me now. And their music.

I know you like reading. Vallès, Zola, Lorca. I ask you to read this diary. When you have time. My dying whines, the ranting and raving of a grumpy old man, the pettiness of my ugly and pathetic existence. It's my requiem, my liturgy. Which I dedicate to you with all my heart. Because today, you see, I am no longer ashamed of belonging to the family of the sick. I am proud of it.

You owe me nothing and I love you very much.

Tuesday 12 March 1940

The Gestapo searched the whole hospital. The beds were turned upside down, the closets pulled apart, the curtains torn. The phonograph in the canteen was broken into a thousand pieces.

They came yesterday, just before I got up. The staff and the patients had to evacuate the premises and go and line up in the courtyard. I didn't even have time to put on a dressing gown. Or even slippers. Two soldiers kept their submachine guns trained on us. Then they brought down the patients from the third floor on stretchers and laid them out on the ground. Dr. Müller tried to talk to them, to demand an explanation. He was struck in the jaw with a rifle butt. I heard the bone crack. They pushed away the nurses who wanted to bandage his wound with a towel. Between the legs of those in the front row, I glimpsed Günter. He was lying against the wall of the covered part of the yard, shivering. I heard them moving the pews in the chapel, pushing the altar across the flagstones. We stayed for a long time in the courtyard, waiting. I felt a strong desire to urinate, because of the cold. Finally, the inspectors came out. They were holding the custodian's son by the elbows. He looked to be bleeding, his eyelids swollen and blistered, like a boxer. His pants were wet. He hadn't been able to hold it in. And then I saw that he wasn't the only one to have wet his pants. I also yielded in the end, seeing the others. The pee warmed me a little at first. Afterwards it's cold. It sticks to your thighs. They called out our names, one by one. Each person lifted his finger in turn and took one step forward. One of the inspectors pointed us out to the custodian's son, who was having difficulty seeing. He looked completely lost. The more they shouted at him, the less he seemed to understand what they wanted of him. I thought about the black market saveloy. Especially when my turn came. But I wasn't afraid. I was actually very calm. I looked the custodian's son straight in the eyes. He was squinting. His right eye was much more swollen than the left. I then looked the inspector straight in the eyes. I couldn't get over the fact that I wasn't afraid. It wasn't sang-froid. Rather a kind of British indifference. A stiff upper lip. A pleasant feeling, given the circumstances. I took one step back. This game lasted all morning. At one point, I raised my head, toward the tops of the plane trees and the sky, completely forgetting what was going on. And then they left with their suspect. I immediately went to Günter, who was still lying on the ground, and asked him how he was. He kissed my hand.

When you come down to it, the Gestapo stopped me from killing myself.

*

I didn't know that I wasn't afraid. I was even sure of the opposite. Until today.

Wednesday 13 March 1940

Surprise visit from Hans's secretary. Hans's ankle still hasn't healed. The young man gave me back my drafts. The articles have been accepted, and the Waffen-SS stamp is there opposite my signature. He gave me a little note from Hans. His famous brass band, which is none other than that of the military district of Salzburg, has started rehearsing the pieces I suggested and which have received the approval of the gauleiter. Clearly, I'm highly rated by the Reich.

Hans is very worried. The brass band has to go to Innsbruck this Saturday night. The famous event will take place somewhere else, he still doesn't know where, the following Monday. Hans will arrive in Innsbruck on Sunday, against his doctor's advice. He asks me, neither more nor less, to replace him in the meantime, if my state of health allows it. Just for one day. He wants to be certain the musicians will be well prepared. He doesn't trust their musical director, a quartermaster always drunk on schnapps. A driver will pick me up and take me to the station. Hans has arranged for my press card to be renewed, signed by the party's cultural attaché. It should be arriving by special courier from Vienna as soon as possible.

It seems to me that Hans has got a nerve. Basically, he's forcing my hand. His secretary certainly wasn't expecting a refusal on my part. I could see that from the expression on his face when I told him I was sorry but I was unable to perform such a service. My excuse was that my doctor had categorically forbidden me to leave the sanitarium, even for a stroll in the city.

*

In the canteen, I found out why the custodian's son was arrested. He'd promised Sapperstein to take care of his old mother and take her something to eat. For months, she'd been hiding in the attic of the disused annex, two streets away. Did Dr. Müller know? Was he the one who informed the Gestapo, as he had with Sapperstein? But that blow with the rifle butt on the jaw . . . Rumors are rife. Some claim that it was the custodian himself who informed on his own son. Since he wasn't arrested. Others speak of a nest egg Sapperstein is supposed to have left so that his mother could be taken care of. And it was the money the cops wanted, not the old lady. But what's the point of speculating? We'll never know.

Again the idea of killing Müller. In case he gets it into his head to inform on me in order to avoid another misplaced rifle butt.

*

Anniversary of the Anschluss. Big concert in Vienna. Speech by Plaschke broadcast on the wireless. *Deutschland über alles* echoed through the dayroom. Grim day. Hymns and marches, oratorios and masses. Why does all this have to happen to music? The instruments should fall silent. The tenors, the violinists. They shouldn't be a party to all this. Out of a sense of decency.

Thursday 14 March 1940
Günter is dead. He caught cold the other day, lying on

the ground in the courtyard. Now it's over, I can forget him.

I didn't go to the morgue. Let alone the funeral. I just thought about the prayer for the dead, the one the Jews recite. I thought about it here, in the chapel. I don't know the Christian prayer either. My father insisted on being cremated. And my mother claimed to be an atheist. It was only for my wife, Maria, that I had to organize a proper funeral. She wasn't angry with God.

*

The custodian's son won't be coming back. There's nobody left to buy me saveloy. Should I ask my tenant?

Friday 15 March 1940
In spite of my refusal, a courier came and gave me my new press card. Bearing the arms of the Reich. Naturally, this valiant messenger clicked his heels. *Heil Hitler!* In front of everyone in Ward 5. I was still in my pajamas.

Salzburg, Wednesday 20 March 1940

M y dear Dieter,
This letter will not be enclosed with the will in
your favor that I have the intention of depositing
with the notary tomorrow and which will reach you by the
intermediary of the consulate of the Reich in Haifa. At least
I hope so.

The tenants of the apartment will be informed of the
identity of their new landlord in due course. You will be free
to sell the property or keep it. If you do not come forward to
claim it, the manager of the sanitarium will be appointed as
sole legatee.

I have just come back from the station in a limousine.
Accompanied by Hans, who has to go to the gauleiter to
make his report. You should see the way the nurses looked
at me. And the others.

I left last Saturday for Innsbruck with the brass band.
With me I had the vial I made up last week. I told myself it
was the ideal opportunity to end with a flourish. Or rather,
with a brass fanfare. To die on a speeding train, while the
countryside rushes by. To breathe my last as I watch a tree
or a meadow disappear into the distance.

I had planned that for the return journey. I didn't want

to embarrass Hans. So I stuffed myself with tonic pills. In order not to die before time.

The journey went well. I was coughing a lot, but the musicians took care of me and gave me hot tea from their thermos flasks. They called me maestro. They laughed and sang throughout the journey. Even the quartermaster, who definitely had one too many. It was lively.

A military truck and a bus were waiting for us at the station in Innsbruck. They took us to the barracks where we would be housed. A substantial meal was served to us in the canteen but I was too exhausted to have any appetite. I went straight to bed and slept as I hadn't slept in ages. In the morning, I went through the scores while the musicians shined their boots and polished their instruments. Then they got their ceremonial uniforms out of their trunks for the dress rehearsal. A disaster. The German marches were passable. But the Italian anthem? A veritable act of aggression. Enough to provoke a vendetta. I did my best to correct the worst mistakes. Without insisting too much. Haven't I already betrayed Mozart? So why fuss over a brass band from Salzburg?

Hans arrived in the afternoon, limping like a wounded mule. He was pale but elegantly dressed. I was pleased to see him. Now I could finally take my train to nowhere. He begged me to go with him to the office of the barracks commander. I was very tired. Noticing that, he took my arm and helped me to walk as one does for an old man, pulling me by the sleeve, encouraging me, even though he was the one who had difficulty walking and stumbled all the time. In the end, I didn't know who was supporting whom. By the time we got to the door of the office, outside which a sentry stood guard, I really thought Hans was going to faint.

Three officers were sitting inside, having a meeting. At the end of the table, a potbellied colonel with pink cheeks and a horrible scar on his forehead. To his left, an SS officer with so many badges, swastikas, skulls, wings and pins of all kinds glittering on his black uniform that I couldn't even tell what rank he was. And on the right, a young special forces lieutenant in camouflage dress. We had to return their Nazi salutes, without losing our balance.

We learned that the ceremony would be taking place the following day at the Brenner Pass. At the actual station on the pass, which is on the Italian border. The Führer was expected to arrive by train early in the morning, in his personal car, at the same moment as the Duce, coming from the Italian side, also by train. It was there that the brass band would come into play for the first time in spite of the noise of the engines. Everything was timed down to the last second.

Lined up like a guard of honor along the central platform between the tracks, the brass band would have to strike up the music as soon as the two trains entered the station and approached at the same dignified speed, Hitler's coming from the north on the left-hand track, Mussolini's coming from the south on the right-hand track. The two trains had to pass each other slowly then draw level, on either side of the central platform, coming to a halt immediately the two official cars were exactly opposite each other. A loud banging of cymbals and drums would mark that solemn moment.

Then the brass band would strike up the national anthems, while the two leaders got off and walked across the platform toward each other, followed by the members of their delegations, shook hands, exchanged a few pleasantries, reviewed the crack corps and climbed into an official car to hold their meeting. Nobody could say how long the audience would last or what the two men would be talking about, with such pomp. And in secret. As soon as they finished, at a signal from the Italian majordomo to the head of the Führer's personal guard, the brass band would start up again and continue playing until the trains had left.

It was at this point that Hans suddenly spoke up. He ran through the program, the list of marches and anthems, pointing out that the judicious choice was due to Herr *Steiner, here present. I was taken aback. I started coughing and couldn't stop. He must have looked like an idiot, our* Herr *Steiner, shaking like an old lady while those hardened soldiers looked on pitilessly. Holding it with the tips of his fingers, the SS officer handed me a white silk handkerchief embroidered with the insignia of his unit. Hans next informed these gentlemen that, given his difficulty in walking, he would require my assistance. He also praised my knowledge of Italian, which might prove useful in case of any last-minute adjustments by the Duce's head of protocol or escort. He even mentioned my invaluable contribution to the preparations for the next* Festspiele *and how well my writings had been received by the gauleiter of Salzburg.*

The fat colonel did not say a word. He merely gave me a respectful smile. The young commando lieutenant said that he had no objection to my presence from a security point of view, as long as a routine check of my antecedents was made. Which was meaningless in the context. The SS officer looked me up and down, rather like Dr. Müller when he examines me, and asked me if I had served in the Austrian army in the last war. I said yes, in the artillery, and that I had been wounded in combat. I straightened my back, and tried to put on a good show, even to smile. You see, Dieter, from that moment on, I did everything I could to put them off the scent. Because I'd made up my mind to go to that damned ceremony. To kill Hitler.

Hans gave a deep bow to the officers, not forgetting the Heil and the salute. I held out the handkerchief for the SS officer to take back, but he refused it. Outside, Hans apologized profusely. He was shaking all over. As was I. I merely thanked him for the honor he was doing me. He seemed a little surprised. But also very relieved. That evening, I stuffed myself with tonic pills. The whole box.

During the night, on the bus ride, I didn't sleep a wink. I watched the stony embankment rush past the window, the better to think. You know me, I'm not the impulsive type. On the contrary, I've always been extremely cautious. I've always taken care not to rush into things, to weigh up the pros and cons before any undertaking. I very much take after my father for that. He wanted at all costs to protect us from imponderables and unknowns, to spare us what he called "unpleasantness." He lived his whole life on the defensive.

Basically, any suicide is a way of bringing an absurd situation to an end. Mine, as was my wont, had all the characteristics of a well thought out, carefully planned act. Logical rather than reckless. In fact, I could have drunk my poisoned potion that night on the bus and watched my life fade away in the darkness, calmly following the course of the stones at the side of the road like a ribbon unwinding. So where did this sudden desire to assassinate Hitler come from? And why the Führer? It was Dr. Müller I really wanted to kill. I never could stand the man.

Kill? It's a funny word. Not at all in my vocabulary. In the end, I couldn't find any plausible reason for my decision.

Not even the pious vow I had taken some time ago. To save Mozart.

*

I've just come back from the canteen. I was hungry. I absolutely must finish this letter. As soon as possible. The chapel is filling with light. Spring is coming. It's been much less cold lately.

*

We got to the Brenner Pass before dawn. The little station was swarming with soldiers and SS. They searched the musicians' trunks, took the trombones to pieces, felt the weight of the drums, checked the passes. My vial was wedged between my press card and the SS man's handkerchief in the inside pocket of my jacket. I was just behind Hans. They pinned badges on our lapels. Our names typewritten on little pieces of card adorned with swastikas. And then they led us to the waiting room. There was coffee and biscuits. The musicians immediately went and took up position on the central platform, between the two frozen tracks. I waited for the fog to lift a little before I joined them. It was bitterly cold. I forgot to put my coat back on when I went out. We rehearsed the most difficult passages and I took the opportunity to look around at the station and watch the comings and goings of the soldiers. I had no idea how to go about it. I considered approaching a soldier, with my respectable air and somber clothes, and grabbing his weapon from him just as the Führer got off the train. But I have no idea how to handle the new submachine guns. They're noth-

*ing like the blunderbusses of the Great War. In any case I
realized that the badge they had pinned on me allowed me
to move about freely. I walked up and down the platform to
warm myself. And to accustom the guards to my presence.*

*Lined up in serried ranks, their backs to the two tracks
running on either side of the central platform, feet together
right on the edge, two cordons of commandos formed a
human barrier. Among them, I recognized the young lieutenant from the day before. The distant whistle of a loco-
motive sounded through the fog. To the north, the Austrian
side. Then, in response, the shriller, closer whistle of the
Italian train climbing the pass. The lieutenant yelled orders
above the din of the approaching engines. The soldiers
immediately stood to attention. Impassive in spite of the
drizzle and the icy wind of morning. I was shivering with
cold, but I made an effort to stand straight and not to cough.
I was so disorientated that I almost forgot to give the signal.
Or was it the quartermaster who gave it in my place?
Whichever of us it was, the band started to play. I heard the
opening tune as if it were coming from the back of a cave.
You see, Dieter, from that moment on, everything happened
as if in a dream. In a mist.*

*The two trains emerged from the fog almost at the same
time, going very slowly. They were covered in flags whose
sharp flapping, joined with the roar of the big engines, covered the sound of the horns and drums. The locomotives
again greeted each other with a few hoots, as they met and
passed in the station. And then, with a hiss, the two trains
came to a perfect halt on either side of the platform. The
Duce's train on the right-hand track, the Führer's on the left.
In the middle, on the platform, the brass band was still playing, shrouded in a mirage of smoke and steam. I could*

hardly breathe. The burning smell of the diesel crushed my lungs and made my eyes smart. Although that also made me look appropriately moved. Some young soldiers also had tears in their eyes, real ones.

Just as I thought I was about to faint, a kind of screaming shook me awake. The song of the trumpets had suddenly become more intense, deafening. Like the shriek of someone being strangled. The two trains formed a sound corridor, trapping the music in their metal vise, perfectly amplifying the effects of the brass and the beating of the bass drum, which the fog had muffled until then. Sustained by this racket pounding in my ears, I recovered. Gradually.

Some SS men in full dress uniform laid red carpets at the feet of the official cars. Italian and German dignitaries were already getting off the other cars. I managed to step back a bit in order not to get caught up in the crush. I even glimpsed Hans at the end of the platform, gesticulating and signaling to me to come back. I was stuck there, huddling against the icy side of the German train. Paralyzed.

The officers quickly took up their positions and everything abruptly froze. The engines fell silent. The clamor of the brass band rose now with ever greater clarity above the platform. The station's sheet metal roof, lined with a ceiling of pine planks, proved excellent for the acoustics, freeing the music from the bottleneck in which the trains had trapped it. I told myself to make a note of that. How good the vibrations were.

An elegant personage in a dark suit got out of the Duce's personal car. He looked like a chamberlain. He came and stood next to me. We were the only two civilians in that sea of uniforms, helmets and plumes. He gave me a friendly nod. I whispered a polite formula in Italian. A high-ranking

Nazi immediately came and shook his hand. Clicking his heels and calling him "my dear count" and "Your Excellency." I recognized him. Graying hair backcombed, stiff back, black jacket like an admiral's, exactly as in the press photographs. Von Ribbentrop. Which meant that the other man, the count, must be his opposite number, Galeazzo Ciano. Ribbentrop glanced briefly at my badge, read my name and, without saying a word, drew his colleague aside. The two Foreign Ministers conversed for about ten minutes, just a few yards from me. Hitler and Mussolini had still not appeared.

My chest was hurting. I needed to clear my throat, to spit. To sit down. My legs were shaking. I leaned on the car. Two huge hands grabbed me by the elbows. Be careful, sir. It was the train driver. He was checking the connecting rods. He wore a tall cap with a black peak and rough leather gloves. An oil can and a dirty cloth were hanging from his belt. He also read my name on the badge and gave a start of surprise. Herr Steiner? He introduced himself in a whisper. My tenant's husband! And then he stiffened. Like a statue.

I turned. Mussolini was standing at the door of his carriage, stretching his arm into the air, as if blessing the men cheering him. On the other side of the platform, Hitler now also appeared. To be greeted by screams of Heil, and the sound of clicking heels, and rifles being shouldered. The horns and percussion of the band, which I had completely forgotten, blared out. Quite emphatic for the Duce. Even louder for the Führer. It was grotesque. An awful pounding. The bad music tore my eardrums. A fairground din. Like those provincial circuses where they beat the drums to announce the entry of the acrobats. All the solemnity of the occasion vanished in one fell swoop. And my fear with it.

Ribbentrop, the count, the SS, the soldiers armed to the teeth, the flags with their garish colors, too long, too big, hanging now at the waxed sides of the trains: it was all like a carnival. So this was History in the making? A scout parade?

Having at last got off the train, the two heads of State advanced slowly toward each other, step by step, as if each feared to be the first to reach the middle of the platform. They embraced, then reviewed the troops. Both were dressed in heavy gabardine coats that came down almost to their ankles. They walked ahead, alone, followed at a distance of some yards by the members of the two delegations. The soldiers stood perfectly still, numb with cold and reverence. Nobody smiled.

The drizzle had turned into fine snowflakes that melted as they ran down my back. My eyes were constantly blinking, because of the wind. However wide I opened them, everything appeared to me as if through a misted window. I felt like a cinemagoer who starts to feel sleepy just as the newsreel comes on and who forces himself to look at a few more images on the screen before dozing off. I discreetly moved away from the ceremony and went and stood by the Italian train, convinced that the talks would take place opposite, in Hitler's personal car. Those few steps were decisive.

I suddenly saw the Führer and the Duce coming straight toward me. Mussolini jutted out his chin at me and, himself holding the door open, invited Hitler to get into the car that was just behind me. The Führer did not seem to notice my presence. He was looking down at the step. I could smell his breath. It smelled of toothpaste. He unbuttoned his coat and moved back the sides to help him climb on. The Duce was waiting patiently for him. Diplomats and officers remained at a respectful distance. Behind them, the officials and soldiers of lesser rank were also heading for other cars, in small groups, or for the waiting room. With one hand, Hitler grasped the handle of the door and, with the other, he held out his officer's cap to me without even turning in my direction. And then he vanished inside. The security cordon drew closer all around me, at the side of the car. The band stopped playing. I stood there on the platform, without moving, Hitler's cap in my hands. The shoulders of my jacket were soaked with snow. The ink on my badge was running to the edge of the card. I tried to mop it with the back of my sleeve, but only succeeded in spreading it. My name was erased. Only the swastika printed at the top, in the corner, remained quite clear and distinct. Opposite, I saw my tenant's husband looking at me, completely dumbfounded.

I don't know how long I stood there like that, as still as a post. My head was empty. I couldn't think. There was nothing left but the cold. And my limbs shivering, my body swaying in the wind, cradled by the squall. I stared stupidly at the gray, damp ground. Was it the concrete of the station or the cement of the covered yard? Somebody came up to me, a majordomo I think, and pointed to a door. I thanked him in Italian. He didn't show any surprise at that. An agent of the Reich to whom the Führer entrusts his headgear must speak several languages. Once inside, I put the cap down on a shelf. I cleaned the edges and the peak with the SS man's embroidered handkerchief. Someone handed me a bowl of hot coffee.

Inside the car, cooks and flunkeys were moving in all directions, their activity supervised by a kind of head waiter. A sumptuous lunch was cooking gently on kerosene stoves.

The aroma of the dishes tickled my nostrils. But my appetite left me as soon as I saw a fellow tasting the food. As in the days of the Borgias. I touched my vial of poison in my jacket pocket. So it was feasible. Almost easy, in fact.

A little bell tinkled briefly. The head waiter hastened to the official car. He returned with an empty coffee pot on a round metal tray. He handed a cup of fresh coffee to the taster. The taster swirled the liquid around in his mandibles as if it were wine. After a few moments, he nodded his consent. The head waiter filled the coffee pot, came very close to me and opened a little cupboard from which he took out a box filled with macaroons, which he then arranged carefully on a plate. He had placed the coffee pot on the shelf, just in front of the Führer's cap. The smell of hot coffee did me good. The little bell rang again, nervously. The head waiter came and stood in front of me, screaming to be brought a carafe of water. It was then that I freed my right hand to reach my vial and pour the contents in the coffee pot. The head waiter turned, the carafe in his hand. I barely had time to lower my arm and close my palm on the vial. He quickly placed the carafe, the macaroons and the coffee pot on a tray. His gestures were jerky. Beads of sweat were forming on his forehead. And then he disappeared at a run into the gangway leading to the next car.

I no longer heard anything but the rapid clumping of his heels. I imagined the two tyrants down there at the end of the corridor, comfortably seated in padded leather armchairs. Nice and snug. Melted snow sliding down the window. The Duce rising. "A little more coffee, mein Führer?" It was while looking at a train window, a landscape rushing past, a tree receding into the distance, that I had wanted to die. The poison in that coffee pot belonged to me. It was for me.

Since the day before yesterday, I've been glued to the wireless set in the covered yard. Hitler hasn't died. Maybe he doesn't like Italian coffee?

With all my love, my dear son. I miss you.

M onday 25 March 1940
Back in a private room!
My tenant's husband has duly paid his rent arrears. I'm sure he's told everyone what he saw at the Brenner Pass. Dr. Müller is waiting on me hand and foot. And so are the nurses. The man who held the Führer's cap! Which also attracts some sidelong glances from the patients.

As a mark of gratitude, Hans has bought me a new phonograph and a few records. Including *Don Giovanni* conducted by Bruno Walter and the unforgettable *Tristan und Isolde* recorded live at the Metropolitan four or five years ago, brilliantly sung by Kirsten Flagstad and Lauritz Melchior. Music has come back. It has been restored to me, in a way.

My new room is bright and very clean. It does smell too strongly of antiseptic, though.

Tuesday 26 March 1940

I have the impression I never left here. Try as I might to conjure up images of the little station, the soldiers, the Führer, the Duce, it's as if I'd never set foot on the Brenner Pass. I still have my press card as evidence. And the washed-out badge. On the other hand, it's only now that I feel the fatigue of that expedition. The tonic pills are no longer any help. I'm exhausted.

*

After the noon meal, I went to the chapel. I met the custodian on my way there. He spat on the ground as I passed.

*

It's up to Salzburg to redeem Mozart. Since it's Salzburg that has betrayed him. The next *Festspiele* is our last chance. Not to save our souls, it's too late for that, but his. And that of the whole of music. Music must be *played*, not *executed*.

I know that neither the custodian's son, nor mine, nor perhaps Sapperstein would have hesitated. But I wasn't ready. This return performance of mine was too abrupt.

I've been living for too long on the margin, cooped up behind hospital walls. Marked with P for Patient on my rump. Like a head of cattle. It's the healthy people, the *normal* people, the SS out there on the streets and in the offices and on the landings, who put me in quarantine, who locked me in this enclosure, out of the way. And, being *sick*, I let them. As if to prove them right.

At first, it was hard, very hard. It still is. An endless apprenticeship, hand to hand combat. For I'm constantly fighting the disease, not submitting to it. The problem is that it has no face, no name. Not even the name Tuberculosis. Even though that's what I live with, day after day. That's what I fight. Without helmet or rifle. It's a serious enemy. Not a tinpot dictator.

Hitler has a name. And a face. Let the healthy serve him

his cup of coffee! Not me. Why should I do their dirty work for them? We *sick* people have enough to do. All alone to face the great nameless, faceless misfortune. Abandoned by everyone. We are already ghosts.

Thursday 28 March 1940
Dr. Müller came to my room to examine me. He was very polite. I think he's a little afraid of me. He hesitated for a long time before asking me why I was praying so much in the chapel. Was it a trap?

According to him, the latest test results are none too encouraging. They're what he calls complications. My lungs took a nasty blow out there on the Brenner Pass. I told him I'd had the feeling things were wrong, that the disease had gotten a bit worse, and that's why I was praying. He seemed to believe me.

It's true that things aren't so good. I looked at myself in the mirror, for a long time. I'd forgotten how pale and thin I am. Like everyone here.

Should I pray, then? I don't know how.

Friday 29 March 1940
Three months to the *Festspiele*. It might as well be three centuries.

Hans sent me an article about Anton Webern. He enclosed a score of his latest composition, a cantata for soprano. The music is too technical, too experimental for me. It reminds me of Schoenberg.

*

I think more and more about my sister and what could have happened to her. It's because it's Friday night, the eve of the Jewish Sabbath. My brother-in-law always respected the tradition, the family meal, the lighting of the candles, the blessing of the bread and the wine. My sister used to laugh about it. Enough to make my father turn in his grave. He was so eager to free us of the burden of religion.

It's dark in the chapel. I'm going to bed.

Monday 1 April 1940
Yesterday morning, excrement left outside my door. It was Sunday. No cleaning woman to clear it up. Today, I complained to the doctor. He's promised to investigate.

Tuesday 2 April 1940
Received rent. My tenant's husband has left again to work in Poland, driving freight trains carrying building material for a big complex near Cracow. A major project.

*

Custodian dismissed. So it was him.

Thursday 4 April 1940
New treatment. Very tired. Breathing difficult.

Strangely, I've stopped thinking about suicide. And about sparing myself further suffering. And yet I'm more and more afraid of death. I can feel it very close, waiting. It mustn't strike before the opening of the *Festspiele* and thwart my plans. It mustn't stop me taking my revenge.

And, if I succeed, finding a way to get this diary to Dieter. Because I want him to know. I want everyone to know.

What exactly does Dieter need to know? Why bother him with this story? The story of how I wasted away. And of a failed assassination attempt. None of the others here are writing their memoirs. What happens to them is of no interest to anyone, and they know it.

Maybe it's best if Dieter doesn't know anything about all this? If he never finds out what happened to us, my sister Gertrude, her husband, her children, me. Isn't it better for him to remember the good old days, when everything was going well? What we really were, before this decline.

Friday 5 April 1940
Cod has again vanished from the menu. And potatoes are rationed. Three per plate. Two if they're big.

The new custodian started work today. He's an invalided ex-soldier. Very young. He has burn scars on his face and one arm has been amputated. A lot more horrible to look at than we consumptives. I asked him to go out and buy me some saveloy or a sausage on the black market. He didn't dare refuse. He knows what happened to his predecessor. Because of me.

He's a country boy, a big strapping fellow from the mountains. Not exactly sharp-witted but pleasant. Jolly even, in spite of circumstances. Nobody else smiles here.

Tuesday 9 April 1940
The black market pork must have been adulterated. Three days of stomach pains, writhing on my bed like an eel. Or is it just that my stomach isn't used to it anymore?

Thursday 11 April 1940
Visit from Hans. He's busy with the preparations for the *Festspiele*. He still needs a helping hand with the editorial aspect. The new cultural officers are worse than the old ones. They were just ignorant brutes. These ones think they're refined. With their black gloves and their clean-shaven faces.

The next festival is shaping up to be a soldiers' cabaret. Hans is irritable. He doesn't look well. He too is reliant on the black market for his food. The grocery stores are empty. You need coupons.

I agreed to help. Not for Hans. But to save Mozart, in spite of everything.

Thursday 18 April 1940
Yesterday evening, speech by Goebbels on the radio, for Hitler's birthday. *Our* Führer is fifty-one. Goebbels voice throbbed. He sounded like an actress in a melodrama. Our old wireless set shook on the little table in the canteen.

Today, we are fighting, keeping our noses to the wheel, that is all. No one complains and no one asks why.

Our people must confront the burdens and difficulties of war. We all resolutely await the Führer's order. When he calls, we will be there.

*

Friday 19 April 1940

I've worked a lot for the *Festspiele* this week. Kept my nose to the wheel, as Goebbels says. I even forgot all about my chest pains. The job exhausts me and sustains me at the same time. It forces me to keep going. Hans's Nazis think I'm making this effort for them, or for fear of them, when in fact it's a matter of survival. I'm clinging on, otherwise I'd slip off and die.

It's only a reprieve, a remission. I'm well aware of that. My fate is being decided hour by hour. The injections are useless. I'm just a specimen for Dr. Müller. A case. For years, he's been keeping a register in which he notes down how long each patient lasts. Hundreds of patients have passed through the sanitarium. Perhaps thousands. Each one is on the list: date of arrival, name, registration number, date of death. Or of recovery.

Dr. Müller would have preferred to work in a research facility, with microscopes and test tubes and glass slides. To have a brilliant career. Discover a serum. I'm more and more convinced that he's experimenting on us. The thing that confirms me in my suspicions is how bad the statistics are here.

Monday 22 April 1940

The name of the new custodian is Stefan. Yesterday, I went to see him in his lodge and we played a game of chess. He's not bad for someone who plays instinctively and doesn't know any of the classic attacks. It reminded me of the good times I had with Günter. I realize now that there was a kind of friendship between us. At the time.

Stefan was wounded in the heavy winter fighting. He's recovered quite quickly. He's from the mountains, strong, accustomed to a hard life. He's not sorry that he fought. I can see he misses the army. Not out of patriotism, no. He liked the atmosphere. And the food, he says. Which makes him laugh because he once spent three days in a trench without any supplies. Not even water. When he was really starving and finally attempted to get away, he realized there was nobody about. His unit had left him there, in the middle of the field. As for his wound, he owes it to a shell that fell short, a German shell. Which also makes him laugh.

*

I'm surprised at my own sociability. With a country boy, to boot. His youth, his laughter, his very roughness, warm my heart. They don't threaten my solitude. They relax me. Like a cigarette or a good glass of wine. I haven't drunk wine for a very long time. I've forgotten the taste.

*

I remember a waterside tavern where I loved to go in spring.

Wednesday 24 April 1940
The doctor has analyzed my last chest X-ray. He looked puzzled. I can see he's a bit surprised at how well I'm holding out. You can imagine how surprised I am! But I think I know why. Vaguely.

Saving Mozart? That's doubtless just an excuse. Killing Hitler? That's all over. What, then? One last bow before the curtain falls? For a single spectator? You, Dieter, my child? Or whoever else finds this diary? Not at all. I'm not leaving a message for posterity. Or confiding secrets. No, it's something quite different. A song, perhaps. Or an arioso? Something to be listened to, in any case.

Moderato cantabile. In D minor. Or C major, it doesn't matter, a score is worthless until it's been played. And mine will be played at the *Festspiele.* That's all I live for. That moment. Not for writing.

Saturday 27 April 1940
We've been left without any care for two days. The staff was kept out in the yard by police inspectors all of yesterday. Part of their investigation, Stefan told me. He wasn't interrogated because the crime in question dates from before he came to the sanitarium. The crime in question?

Stefan ran to tell everyone, at the request of the inspectors: the patients are forbidden to leave their rooms until further orders.

Monday 29 April 1940
The search came as a surprise on Saturday, in the middle of the night. It lasted for hours. I hid my notebook on the window sill, jammed under the shutter.

Two men came in without knocking. It must have been three or four in the morning. They banged on the walls, tore out the skirting boards, took my phonograph apart. I stood in a corner. Barefoot. In my pajamas. I didn't dare move. Or even look at them.

They didn't find anything. They told me to stay in my room and I would be summoned later, if necessary. I kept standing there in the corner of the room until dawn.

The vial! Where had I put the vial with the poison? I couldn't remember. Had it been found and analyzed?

Yesterday, Sunday, the comings and goings continued. We weren't given anything to eat or drink. I considered running away. Impossible. Especially in my condition. Where would I have gone anyway? I waited for hours. Staring at the door. Listening out for every sound. Why didn't they come?

This morning, Stefan told us the investigation was over and we could go down to the canteen. Everyone was anxious to know what had happened. The manager came in, followed by the staff. He informed us that Dr. Müller had been arrested after the previous custodian had informed on him. For drug trafficking. Müller had been selling our medicines to a gang of crooks. On the black market. We were being treated with aspirin, in tablet or powdered form, and with paracetamol diluted in water for the injections. Hence the statistics.

In the medicine cabinet, there was nothing but improvised mixtures. Sugar, flour, fruit syrup, dyes. Even turpentine. Nothing that could cure us. Or kill Hitler.

Thursday 2 May 1940
Received rent. The manager took most of it. To treat us with aspirin? He told me how difficult it is to balance the books, as if that were any concern of mine. Dr.

Müller's felony has given the sanitarium a bad reputation. The few well-to-do patients have left without settling their bills. They're threatening legal action. Neither the ministry nor the municipality wants to keep subsidizing this outpost for the dying. Because of the war effort. Consequently, the management is finding it hard to raise the funds to supply the sanitarium with medicines and is being forced to dismiss a large number of staff. Starting this month, the patients will have to do their own cleaning and wash their own dirty linen with soap. Food will be rationed and limited to only what is strictly necessary. In these conditions, impossible to find a new doctor. Not even a student. Nobody wants anything to do with this wretched place. Or us. I can perfectly well understand that.

*

Yesterday, the Japanese cancelled the Olympic Games that were due to be held in Tokyo. The sportsmen are disappointed. Fortunately, the *Festspiele* will still take place.

Tuesday 7 May 1940
Unbearable atmosphere. What a shambles! Everywhere filth is piling up. I shut myself up in my room, which I keep clean and tidy. I've put the skirting boards torn out by the policemen under my bed and I've repaired the phonograph. I listen to my three remaining records all day long. The patients hang about in the corridors, on the stairs, in the courtyard. Even those from the third floor, who've stopped washing. I pretend there isn't that con-

stant coming and going on the other side of the door, that shuffling of slippers on the tiles. Where are they all going?

*

Finally left my room this afternoon. A game of chess with Stefan, in his lodge. I won as usual. He keeps smiling in spite of everything. I envy him. He's convinced it'll all be sorted out sooner or later and we'll get back to normal. We drank schnapps. Real rotgut. It was good.

Thursday 9 May 1940
Hans came to see how I was. The festival's getting closer. Articles and programs have to be *corrected* before leaving for the printer. I have to make a few changes. My notes for the opening of the *Kultursommer* are lacking in enthusiasm, apparently. And I've used too many technical terms in introducing the works.

The choice of the various compositions leaves me somewhat skeptical. I can't detect any connecting thread, any particular theme, in this symphonic medley. Who chooses the pieces to be played? Goebbels himself? Hans has no idea. All he knows is that "it's been decided at a high level."

The event is intended to demonstrate a sense of renewal, the determination of the Reich to produce works of art that are healthy, vigorous, free of the moods and depression in which today's decadent creators wallow. A wild, imposing lyricism holds sway under the batons of Böhm, Furtwängler, and Lehár. A kind of heightened, and very Teutonic, romanticism.

Curiously, Karajan won't appear at the *Festspiele*. A big

concert in Berlin, Hans told me. Karajan is Hitler's protégé, after all. Not the protégé of the Austrian gauleiters.

*

Hans had the good grace not to mention the deteriora-
tion of the sanitarium. Or mine. But, once our conversa-
tion was over, I could see how happy he was to be getting
back to the outside world.

Saturday 11 May 1940
Very proud of myself. I couldn't stand it anymore. I was
stifling. I shaved and dressed and went out for a stroll.
This year, spring is radiant. It was hard to walk but I managed to get to the center of town. To mingle with the
crowd, to stroll on the streets, to look in the shop windows, to sip a lemonade at a kiosk. It was ecstasy!
I didn't meet any of my old acquaintances, which was
fine by me. The strangers I passed were extras. They were
part of the decor, just like the trees, the sparrows, the
benches. A moving tableau, almost unreal. Soldiers rolling
cigarettes and whistling at the girls. Children playing hop-
scotch. The tinkling of bicycle bells. A bricklayer at work.
An old gentleman raising his hat to me in greeting, old
style. A big dog dozing in a doorway. I considered going
all the way home and saying hello to my tenant, who's
pregnant. And then I saw a Star of David whitewashed on
a shop, with the word *Juden* in the middle, and decided to
turn back.

Tuesday 14 May 1940
A solution has been found. Part of the sanitarium will be turned into a convalescent home for soldiers. The hospitals are overflowing with wounded. Once they've been treated, those without families or anywhere to go will be transferred here until they're well enough to leave. An army doctor is expected soon.

*

The panzer regiments massed in Belgium have crossed the Meuse and are now making for France. The Luftwaffe is bombing Rotterdam. The Queen of Holland has escaped. The Polish Jews have been rehoused in ghettos. Still no announcement about the *Festspiele*. I have a horrible feeling it may be cancelled at the last minute. Like the Olympic Games. I never imagined the war would be on such a scale.

I keep writing in spite of everything. Hans has promised that I'll be remunerated.

Thursday 16 May 1940
My father was right, at the end of the day, to want to convert.

Friday 17 May 1940
Workers have come and left ladders, buckets and bags of cement. They're starting work on Monday.

Saturday 18 May 1940

Again thought about my father. And mother. It's from them that I get my love of music. My sister always preferred painting. The Impressionists. Especially the women, Berthe Morisot, Mary Cassatt, Suzanne Valadon. She used to visit Viennese galleries, auction rooms, art bookshops. She'd drag her husband along. Even the children sometimes. But you, my son, haven't an esthetic bone in your body. Politics, on the other hand, is in your blood. Marx, Engels, Kropotkin. You chose your side, the way an artist chooses his school.

I've never followed any movement. That's what my father bequeathed to me, however reluctantly: non-belonging. I'm neither a Jew nor a non-Jew. And that's partly his fault.

*

This evening, I continued with my reminiscences. I remembered your childhood, and mine. Before all these choices. The ones you made. The ones I could have made.

Monday 20 May 1940

The work has started. The workers sing to themselves amid the din of hammers and saws and drills. An operetta for voices and tools, with the foreman, a noisy, efficient Tyrolean, as solo tenor. The corridors already smell new. Stefan runs all over the place. He's very busy. He jokes with everyone. He gets along well with these fellows who come from the outskirts of town or, like him, from the country.

*

The noise helps me work. I imagine I'm hearing the stage hands and prop men at the opera, putting up a set.

I've reworked the press release for the opening of the festival, putting in the necessary flourishes. High-flown expressions, exclamation marks, emphatic adverbs. Not difficult. A bit like the effects in the Führer's speeches. To show off, to impress the masses. I found it quite amusing to plagiarize Nazi bombast.

*

This evening, I reread what I'd written. It's pure nonsense.

Wednesday 22 May 1940
Bronchial tubes congested for the past two days. All that plaster dust.

I considered going out, sitting on a bench, getting some fresh air. Too weak. My disease is trying to regain the upper hand. How to stop it? Even Mozart couldn't manage that, despite the fact that music still needed him.

I know I'm not going to save the *Festspiele* with my articles. Everything is checked and censored anyway. The finest works will be slaughtered. Even Mozart. I can already see Böhm and Lehár wielding their batons like clubs. So what can I do?

*

Salzburg won't be Bayreuth. Anything but that!

ʎ

Thursday 23 May 1940
Not good.

Friday 24 May 1940
Stefan worried. He brought me some soup which he got from one of the workers. With pieces of bacon in it. I remembered the taboo against eating the meat of the pig. Why pigs and not cows?
I thought about God. But that's because I'm sick. I've never felt as helpless as I do now. It's as if the disease had me in a judo hold and was keeping me down on the carpet, my shoulders on the ground.
I fight against sleep. For fear that I won't wake up again. I write and write. So as not to fall asleep. *This year's* Festspiele *will go down in history. It is the first great artistic event of a new civilization on the rise, in Salzburg, in Berlin, in Munich and throughout the Reich. A civilization that unites us all! Thanks to the miracle of radio broadcast, the music of Mozart will be heard in millions of homes and will echo throughout the world. Henceforth, our lives will be lived to his rhythms. The same music for everybody!*
This year's Festspiele *will go down in history. The organizers have done everything possible to . . .*
The SS love music the Führer loves music the Teutons the Italians the Blacks plants and babies love music the radio loves music loves

Tuesday 28 May 1940
Slightly better. First visit from the new doctor. Young. In an impeccable uniform. No white coat. He looked through my file, examined me without a word, made a few notes and left to continue his rounds. A very medical visit. Müller may have been a crook and a hypocrite, but he was always friendly with the patients. Straight too. He came right out with his diagnosis, without kid gloves. He at least pretended to be treating us. And he wore a white coat.

Thursday 30 May 1940
The army convalescents will be here in two weeks. I'll have to vacate my room. As I still have no idea where I'll be moved to, I simply threw the bare essentials in a traveling bag. Whatever I can't keep with me Stefan will store in the cellar. There's a feeling of departure, like in a station. Everyone is a bit disorientated. We patients are not accustomed to moving fast like soldiers. And without arguing. Some tug at the lieutenant's sleeve and bombard him with stupid questions. Which annoys him. I can understand that. This lack of discipline doesn't do us credit. It infuriates me.

Friday 31 May 1940
I listened to the arias from *Così fan tutte*, conducted by Fritz Busch, three times in succession, then wrapped my records and my phonograph in newspaper.

*

Impossible to get a wink of sleep. A lot of hustle and

bustle. Furniture being shifted, doors slamming, hurried footsteps on the stairs and, outside, truck engines running. I don't dare go see.

Saturday 1 June 1940
The third floor was evacuated last night. In one fell swoop. Nobody knows where the patients have been taken. Not even Stefan. It transpires that we're all going to be rehoused up there. The first and second floors will be for the soldiers. We'll have our meals in our rooms. The orderlies are spraying the wards with antiseptic. But what about the mattresses?

Sunday 2 June 1940
Tired out by all this upheaval. Not strong enough to go for a walk in town. I went down to the courtyard. I listened to the birds chirping in the trees. Sitting on a bench, in the sun. There were two other patients, their backs against the wall, talking excitedly about the move. Thanks to them, I couldn't hear the sparrows.

Inside, the place is a hive of activity. It's a bit grotesque, all this commotion. A storm in a teacup, as the English say.

Tuesday 4 June 1940
I'm in Ward 9A, next to the stairs. Twelve beds, with hardly any space between them. The man in the bed on my right is about fifty, tidy, quite friendly, and has clearly decided to make the best of a bad job. The one on my left is much older, and seems slightly senile. He doesn't talk

much, spends most of his time lost in thought. Both have one unpleasant characteristic in common. They snore.

A single wash basin. Shower and toilets on the landing. Rusty bars on the windows. But some attempts at decoration all the same. A crucifix above the door. A few photographs on the wall. Riverside views, vineyards, mountain peaks.

Like the others, I've arranged my family photographs on the shelf we have instead of a night table. I've put everything else under my bed. My diary is now among my socks. But I've been given permission to place my phonograph on a linen shelf in the corridor, which has become our drawing room, our boulevard, our café terrace.

People are organizing themselves as best they can. There's even a corner of the landing reserved for those who want a bit of privacy. That was decided spontaneously and by tacit agreement.

No more radio. The wireless has stayed downstairs in the canteen. Thank goodness for that.

Thursday 6 June 1940
No news from Hans. A pity, because I've finished my work. I'm waiting for him. This month's rent is still unpaid, according to the manager. Revolting food. Dust everywhere. Stefan says everything will be better when the soldiers arrive.

I feel a kind of depression.

Friday 14 June 1940
Arrival of the war wounded at the sanitarium. Great upheaval. Stefan is very excited. We're confined to our floor until further orders.

I had expected shouting and laughter, the clumping of boots. I stood at the top of the stairs, listening hard, but everything happened in silence. I find it hard to believe they're there, just downstairs.

Saturday 15 June 1940

Hans was finally able to come! I received him in our *drawing room*. He brought me some cookies in a bag. And a few food coupons. My wages as a music critic.

The *Festspiele* will take place as planned. For two whole weeks! From 13 to 29 July. That's in less than a month! Hans has promised to get me tickets. He glanced at my corrections and patted me on the back, smugly. Seeing me looking so pale, he probably doesn't think I'll last until the festival. I can't stop coughing, I can hardly breathe, but I'll be there. Just whispering the dates, *13 to 29 July*, gives me strength. The dates reverberate in my head like pealing bells. No more depression. Enough of this moaning. Otto, my dear fellow, the *Festspiele* awaits you! You have an appointment with Mozart!

I told Hans about the arrival of the soldiers yesterday, to explain my sudden transfer to the third floor. As if to apologize. His only reply was to tell me that the troops of the Reich had entered Paris. Also yesterday.

*

I feel much better this evening. A beautiful, glowing sunset through the windows. Spring at last.

Sunday 16 June 1940
Paris has fallen. I can't believe it.

Monday 17 June 1940
New menu. Army rations. But they're only scraps left over from the meals downstairs, just a bit reheated and served to us from a big cauldron.

We're still not allowed to go downstairs. In order not to contaminate the wounded. The filth doesn't help. Litter is piling up. The staff can't cope. No time to devote to us civilians. We smell bad.

Stefan is quite disappointed. The newcomers are either horribly crippled or in a state of shock. In a really bad way, he told me. In other words, not very good company.

I surprised Stefan by telling him that I might have *Festspiele* tickets for him. The fact is, I want him to go with me. To support me in case my strength fails. I have no desire to collapse in front of everyone in the middle of a concert hall.

And I'll need an accomplice.

Wednesday 19 June 1940
The man on my left is fading fast. He keeps muttering incomprehensibly. Or rather, not so much muttering as singing, in a kind of Germanic dialect but with a slightly softer, more Slavonic intonation. The tune is always the same, quite a lively one. Probably a folk dance. I could write an article about it, an essay. *Music and memory.* Or even a short piece of music. *Wind sonata for consumptive lungs.*

*

Friday 21 June 1940
Stefan came up to see me. We chatted about this and that.
The weather, the war, his work. And then, fleeing the noisy
corridor, we played a game of chess on my bed. The old man
was snoring softly. After a moment, he took a deep breath, as
if suffocating. We thought he was giving up the ghost, but he
suddenly started singing to himself. Stefan listened, a slight
smile at the corners of his mouth. He looked at me hesitantly.
I realized that he'd recognized the song the old man was
muttering. At last he made up his mind. It's *Jewish*, he said,
proud to display his expertise. I found it hard to conceal my
surprise. There were some Jews in his village. Six families.
One of them was the blacksmith. They sang like that, in bad
German, whenever they got together for a feast day or a
wedding. One of them would accompany the others on the
violin and tap his feet. When the weather was nice, you'd see
them dancing together in the blacksmith's yard.

*

A Jew, here? So close to me?

Saturday 22 June 1940
We've been punished, like little boys. Deprived of
meals. And visits. The lieutenant is very angry. Someone
from our floor went down to the second floor to look for
soap, apparently. The lieutenant gave him a thrashing and
threw him out of the sanitarium.

Monday 24 June 1940
Punishment over. Those who can are even allowed to go out, but not by the stairs. A ladder has been placed at the back of the building. We just have to ask Stefan. He raises it and places it up against the façade, so that it reaches the window in the corridor. The man on my right was the first to go out for a walk, today. I gave him a note to deliver to Hans. He brought back a handful of acid drops. He gave me a lemon-flavored one.

My note to Hans was a comment on the second concert of the *Festspiele.* It's a heavy program. To start the Tchaikovsky symphony immediately after the concerto, without transition, strikes me as too abrupt. The effect will be to crush Mozart and turn his concerto into a mere interlude. Right there in the Mozarteum! Wolfgang Schneiderhan will be the violinist. Why not take advantage of his virtuosity and let him play a short solo between these two long and contrasting works? It'll make for a more flexible whole, and add a touch of refinement.

*

The lieutenant came to do his tour of inspection. He reminded us of the rules, the importance of hygiene. No contact with the men on the second floor. I had the impression he was embarrassed, even ashamed. In my opinion, he doesn't want us—or anyone else—to see these war wounded.

Tuesday 25 June 1940
I asked Stefan to tell me about the Jews in his village. My father never told us anything about his family, or about

his life in Silesia. He had a strong foreign accent that amused us greatly, especially when he tried to adopt a more distinguished tone, Viennese style. We all knew he could speak perfect Yiddish. But he never uttered a single word, not even in his sleep.

Stefan didn't have much to tell. When he was little, he played with them, in the fields. He even learned some bad language. *Ein groïss dreck*. And then, as he grew, he kept only professional relations with them. Especially with the blacksmith. At least until he left for Palestine. *Das helige Land*, as Stefan calls it. He even has his address, somewhere in Galilee. The Jew entrusted him with his equipment and his tools, saying he would find a way to have them sent to him by boat. But he still hasn't been in touch even though it's been more than three years since he left. The others also left, but later. Just a few months ago. From one day to the next, they were gone.

I find it absurd that a peasant from the mountains should know so many Jews, whereas, apart from my brother-in-law and my nephews, I myself have never rubbed shoulders with any. Just a few musicians, one or two composers, at festivals. Professional relations, as Stefan says.

*

Drew a little calendar, with boxes and borders, to mark the days still remaining until the *Festspiele*.

I hope Hans will take my suggestion seriously. I'd so much like to be there that evening. It will probably be my last lap. After that . . .

What else do I have to hold on to?

Friday 28 June 1940
Hitler is visiting Paris. He was very impressed by the Opéra. So am I. I went to a wonderful performance of *Carmen* there. With my wife. Afterwards, we went for a meal at the *Petit Riche*. Very expensive and very good. And then made love for a long time in our hotel room at the foot of the Butte Montmartre.

Saturday 29 June 1940
The old man in the bed to my left is going completely off the rails. He again did his business in the sheets. I whispered in his ear: Calm down, today's your Sabbath. *Shabbes, shabbes.* He didn't react.

We had to wash him ourselves, and his sheets, because of the smell. Should I inform on him just to get him out of here? I'm not even sure he is a Jew. I saw him naked as we were washing him. He isn't circumcised.

But then neither am I.

*

This overcrowding is becoming frankly intolerable. There's no demarcation, as there was before, between the dying and the others, the old and the young, the incurables and the convalescents. To tell the truth, I don't belong to any of these categories. I'm neither young nor old and not completely moribund. I live in troubled waters. Like a pebble in a stream. A pebble that's still rolling.

Tuesday 2 July 1940
Impossible to sleep. The old man in the next bed is delirious. Between the spluttering and the wheezing, he endlessly sings the same tune. Hour after hour. It's unbearable.

Wednesday 3 July 1940
Exhausted. I didn't sleep a wink last night. The old man didn't stop singing his song for a single minute. The same tune, again and again. I nudged him with my elbow, tapped him on the cheek. I even considered smothering him with a pillow. And then I collapsed with exhaustion on my bed. Doomed to listen to his groaning.

After a while, I noticed that the song was helping him to breathe. It was getting the air to circulate in his mouth. If he'd fallen silent, his lips would have closed and his throat would have been paralyzed. It struck me as a good technique, a breathing exercise. So I took up the tune, in canon, then the guttural noises, in my father's accent. Very low. Gradually, it cleared my lungs too. And calmed me a little.

Now I can't get it out of my head!

Thursday 4 July 1940
Received a kind note from my tenant. She's entering the sixth month of her pregnancy, and is sorry she can't come to see me. Because of the germs. She apologizes for the delay in settling the rent. She hasn't seen her husband in several weeks. The railway company is only paying a meager wage by transfer. The rest consists of small bonuses,

paid directly in cash to each train crew. All she knows is
that he was hospitalized for a few days in Poland. The doctors were afraid he might have caught typhus or something
like that. Luckily, that turned out not to be the case. Just a
bad bout of flu.

She asked me if I'd agree to be the baby's godfather.
Even though I can't come to the christening. I cried for the
first time in ages.

Friday 5 July 1940
Visit from Hans. He's a brave man.

We had to take refuge on the landing. Because of the
old man's constant muttering. And the filth. We didn't talk
either about my illness or about the war. There's nothing
to be said about either of them.

The *Festspiele* begins in a week. Hans brought me two
tickets for the second concert, which will be held at the
Mozarteum. Stefan will be able to go with me. Or rather to
support me. I'm getting weaker by the day. There's nothing I can do about it. The other performances don't interest me at all. Not even the gala evening: Beethoven's
Leonore Overture and Bruckner's Seventh. God, how old
hat it all is. How unoriginal.

I can already hear the Festspielhaus echo to the
applause of gloved hands. I see the auditorium, the gilded
molding, the crystal chandeliers, and sitting there in rows,
the over-starched dress uniforms, the bourgeois in their
tails, the young aristocrats in their Gatsby-style clothes
with their mistresses, the old countesses snoring, the SS
officers strutting on the mezzanine, the bespectacled aca-
demicians, and all that Austro-Hungarian rabble still

stinking of the Black Forest, however swankily they present themselves. I know them all. I was one of them. How much hair cream, shoe polish, eau de toilette and silk handkerchiefs did I have to use to go and listen to music? War paint.

The cultural committee has carefully chosen the pieces. Popular operas, easy pieces for flashy virtuosos, regional music, and waltzes, lots of waltzes. Admittedly, the audience will consist mostly of military personnel. Which makes it all the more surprising that my suggestion has been taken seriously. Hans says Schneiderhan is delighted at the idea of performing alone on stage, unaccompanied. The gauleiter has no objection, provided the piece is short. No more than five or ten minutes. And that's the snag. Schneiderhan can't decide. He'd like to do something impressive, to stand out. He's afraid there's a danger this little interlude will go unnoticed, wedged as it will be between two major works, crushed by their power. I told Hans we needed something lively, something, ideally, that would get the audience to join in and clap their hands in time to the music. I should have kept my mouth shut. Hans immediately asked me to advise him on the question.

The Mozart concerto comes just after the opening piece, the awful *Salzburger Hof- und Barockmusik* by Jerger, as Teutonic as anyone could wish—the whole thing cheerfully hammered home by Böhm's conducting—and just before Tchaikovsky's Fourth Symphony. They couldn't have murdered Mozart better if they'd tried. Or the very soul of Salzburg. What a capitulation! I feel ashamed. As an Austrian. It makes the Americans at the Cosmopolitan Opera, or even the French, look good. Not because they play better. But because they have a sense of decency. And the minimum amount of humility needed to perform such great music.

So I'll have five minutes to save Mozart. It's all I need. Not with a cup of coffee. Or with a vial full of poison. But with music, as is only fitting. Using a violin.

Five minutes is a lot. Killing Hitler would only have taken thirty seconds.

Sunday 7 July 1940

I've got it! I've found the perfect piece. I just have to transcribe it and arrange it for violin. It's unlikely that Hans would find a score in the library of the Academy. In any case I prefer to adapt it to suit Wolfgang Schneiderhan. He'll be more inspired if the rhythm matches his style of playing. As the young prodigy he is, he'll know how to give it the right fire and passion. I trust him. He'll be eager to shine.

Stefan is very excited at the thought of going with me. He's never set foot in a concert hall. Or attended an event at which high society will be present.

He's found a suit that fits him in the storeroom next to the morgue. A little threadbare but presentable. Stefan won't look out of place among the soldiers, with his amputated arm and his scars. I'll lean on his remaining arm. What a fine pair! A consumptive and a disabled ex-serviceman.

Tuesday 9 July 1940

A courier came yesterday to take the score. It's written on medical prescriptions. I had no spare paper of the right format. Stefan wasn't able to get me anything better from the management. He also brought me a ruler and some ink. I worked the whole of Sunday night, in the corridor. I hummed the tune a hundred times in a low voice, writing it down note by note. Repeating the melody, and exaggerating the rhythm.

Now, it's only a matter of waiting.

Wednesday 10 July 1940

The doctor doesn't know I'm going to the concert. I told him I'd been invited to dinner by an old acquaintance who lives not far from here. He didn't believe me. The patients always make lame excuses in order to go out. The doctor isn't taken in. He knows perfectly well that most go to find food on the black market or to visit a brothel in the lower town. He understands, he's a soldier.

*

France has a new government. Led by Pétain. I remember that name. "The victor of Verdun!" To each his own betrayal. We betray Mozart. He betrays Ravel and Debussy. Does the Marshal have a baton, like Böhm?

Friday 12 July 1940

Revolting food. I'd never have imagined I'd one day have a craving for cod. Even boiled. Sapperstein wouldn't touch meat. Out of respect for tradition. Should I envy him for staying true to himself right to the end? For holding out in spite of everything?

My father couldn't see any good reason to remain a Jew. And plenty of bad ones. Of course, he was quite right. If he hadn't been, those who came looking for Sapperstein would have taken me away too.

Sapperstein didn't put up any resistance to the Gestapo men. He didn't even try to lie, to argue, to offer a bribe. The only thing he insisted on was not eating meat. Not swallowing impure food. And yet he wasn't religious. I think he was actually a Trotskyite.

My father loved *Schweinfilet* and diced bacon. Not my mother, because it's fattening. Nor my sister, because of her husband. Or just to annoy father. It was her way of being revolutionary. Or reactionary? In any case, father forgave her everything.

Where is she now? Where are the children?

*

What about Dieter? Is he still in Palestine? I very much doubt it. Zionism, agriculture, draining marshes. It's not for him. He isn't a Jew, after all. He always wanted to be a citizen of the world. Stateless. Rootless. That was his idea of freedom.

I remember the family arguments before Dieter went off to join the anti-Fascists in Spain. My brother-in-law was outraged. He called my son a Bolshevik, the black sheep of the family. Dieter loved that. And to think we'd dreamed of his becoming a teacher. Even a university professor. He would have stayed here in Salzburg. He would have come to see me, his briefcase under his arm, stuffed with books.

*

Basically, I'm the only member of the family who doesn't belong to anything. Who hasn't made a choice. What group do consumptives subscribe to? What ideology? The seriously ill are also a caste. A very egalitarian one. But on what side are they? Do they have a program?

My nationality is Austrian, my denomination consumptive. And I'm proud of it . . .

Saturday 13 July 1940
Opening of the *Festspiele*!

Sunday 14 July 1940
Very tired. No news from Hans. He must be snowed under with work. Did he even glance at the score? The second concert is in three days.

Stefan brought me some hot tea. I told him not to worry. We'll go to the Mozarteum. On a stretcher if need be! I wouldn't miss it for the world. My last *Festspiele*. Before I become like the old man in the next bed.

He's stopped singing his little song. But I can't get it out of my head. It's always there, like a virus. One that he's passed to me.

*

It's incredibly quiet. I like it. The days here are all the same. Coughing, filth, depression. But Sunday is a magical day. Even for us. Just because it's Sunday.

For the Arabs, it's Friday, and the Jews, Saturday. The three together make what the Americans call a long weekend.

Monday 15 July 1940
More than two days. Still no news from Hans.

The Mozart violin concerto is already stroking my eardrums. I quiver with pleasure. I imagine the rehearsals, the conductor's admonitions, the stage hands disturbing everything. I hear every stroke of the bows, every breath of the brass, even the rustling of paper when the musicians turn their pages. It does me enormous good.

Gradually, the old man's tune has withdrawn into the wings. I've stopped hearing it. Even in my head. And the old man hasn't started singing it again. He sleeps all the time, with his fists clenched, like a little boy. Curled up.

Stefan continues to bring me tea to buck me up. But it's Mozart who keeps me warm. The violin concerto.

Tuesday 16 July 1940
The old man died during the night. Without a word. Without waking us. He should never have stopped singing. Falling silent clogged his bronchial tubes.

Stefan and one of the patients rolled him in his dirty sheet and took him down to the morgue. He didn't weigh much. His bed is empty for the moment. Curiously, the tune has come back. It stops me from hearing the concerto. A bit like interference on the wireless. It's obvious the old man won't leave me in peace, even now that he's dead.

*

Stefan came back this evening to see how I was. He told me a distant cousin of the dead man came to take the body. He's going to see to the funeral arrangements. And the old man wasn't a Jew, Stefan laughed. His cousin is a country priest. He placed a rosary in the old man's hands just before the undertakers took him away on a cart covered with a black cloth. But then why was he always singing a Jewish song? There was no lack of songs in our villages. Or Jews, said Stefan. That's why we made them clear out. We were tired of listening to them. And he burst out laughing.

*

A Christian is a Jew who's out of his mind.

*

I'll die singing Mozart to myself. Artur Rubinstein will die singing Chopin. What will Karajan be singing? Strauss and Beethoven. What about Goebbels? Or Hitler? But they aren't musicians.

Wednesday 17 July 1940
The great day! I have a shave, then get all dressed up and strut in front of the mirror in the corridor. My suit is much too big on me. I look like an adolescent who's stolen his old uncle's jacket. Being thin makes me look younger. If only I weren't so pale. My skin is all creased. I hope I don't meet anyone I know.

Could anyone really recognize me? I used to be a bit on the large side, with pink cheeks. I held myself erect, with my head up. In the old days.

Stefan doesn't want to get dressed before going out. He's waiting until the last minute for fear of ruining his clothes. He spent the night brushing them and slept on his pants so that the mattress would give them a perfect crease. He sewed the sleeve on the side of his missing arm to the pocket of the jacket. How does he do all that with just one hand?

It's almost time. I'm afraid I won't make it, that I'll collapse on the way. Or have to leave the hall before the end of the concert. I ought to have tonic pills, brandy, hot tea. I haven't eaten a thing since yesterday. I have a lump in my throat.

I think . . . The stairs. I can hear Stefan . . .

M y beloved son,
I really hope this letter reaches you one day.
Wherever you are.

Stefan is angry with me. We've fallen out. He came to fetch me yesterday, late in the afternoon. It was hard for me to walk. The air outside made me dizzy. After an hour, he hailed a taxi. Which he had to pay for out of his own pocket. I'd forgotten my wallet. In my excitement. We arrived earlier than we'd anticipated. Well before the start of the concert. Security was very tight. I said that Stefan was my personal nurse, to impress the policemen. Then I said I was a guest of Hans. They didn't react. So I told them the gauleiter was waiting to thank me for my help in organizing the Festspiele. As evidence, I quoted by heart the introduction I wrote for the evening's program. A detective checked in the brochure that's distributed on the way in. He briefly saluted me and finally let us pass. I was shaking. Not with fear or with cold. Just from having been standing for so long.

Stefan was struck dumb. The gold leaf on the ceiling, the red carpet, the polished brass handrails. We sat down on the mezzanine landing. The guests started to fill the lobby. Officers in gray, in black, in the royal blue of the air force

*and a few white navy uniforms. The peaks of their caps
shone in the light of the chandeliers. The SS carried ceremonial knives at their sides. Everyone was talking loudly, tapping each other on the shoulder, chain smoking. I thought I
was going to choke.*

*A few rank and file soldiers stood in a corner. Intimi-
dated. Some had bandaged heads, others crutches. Heroes.
And then the dignitaries from the various government
departments made their entrance. The gauleiter rapidly
shook a few hands, gave a few generalized salutes and* Heil
Hitlers *and went straight up to the royal box. No big shots
from Berlin or Munich. Lots of Viennese, on the other hand.
Looking both elegant and ill at ease. Lost in a sea of uniforms.*

*Stefan and I quickly went to our seats to avoid the rush
that always ensues when the bell rings to announce the
beginning of a concert. Fifteenth row, on the left. I hate
being in the middle. It makes me feel too conspicuous. I prefer the seats right at the end of the row, near the aisles,
which make me feel as though I have a view of backstage.
And it means having just one neighbor instead of being
stuck between two.*

*Stefan sat down to my right. I could sense how nervous
he was. He kept crossing and uncrossing his legs as if he
didn't know what to do with them. I think he would have
liked to be able to fold them and put them in his pocket. To
calm him down, I explained the program, pointed out what
to listen for, and above all advised him not to applaud at the
ends of movements. Only when the piece is over and the
conductor turns to receive his ovation. I stupidly forgot that
he had only one arm. He didn't point out my blunder.*

After the ritual of tuning up, the scores being steadied on the music stands, and the last coughs, Böhm made his entrance. Stefan was on the verge of getting to his feet and standing to attention. I had to tug at his sleeve to hold him back. The poor fellow was too tense to take advantage of that magical atmosphere one always finds in a concert hall just before a performance. But as soon as the music started, he was spellbound, hypnotized even. Not me. I can't stand Jerger. So heavy-handed! Such kitsch! Superficial lyricism without any passion, baroque effects laid on thick like whipped cream on a Viennese pastry.

And then it was Mozart's turn. I wept. With joy. And with anger. Our Mozart! Not theirs. Böhm gave a good account of himself and Schneiderhan was in fine form. Inspired. His violin led the orchestra with confidence. Böhm had the good grace to move aside and let the young virtuoso give free rein to his enthusiasm. It wasn't out-standing, no, but it was convincing. A fine display of skill. Take it or leave it. I was happy to take it. I clapped as hard as everyone else. And Stefan cheered as only a boy from the mountains can do. Loudly enough to bring the chandeliers down. Imagine my surprise when Schneiderhan came back on stage, without Böhm, and, having called for silence, announced that he was going to play a short solo. So Hans had read the score and the committee had agreed to its being performed, just as I had suggested. To mark the end of the concerto less abruptly, to keep the atmosphere going a little longer before the intermission, before Tchaikovsky. To save Mozart!

Without further ado, the first lively chords sounded, and the audience seemed delighted. Except for Stefan who craned his neck as if he was having difficulty hearing. Schneiderhan was winning his wager. The audience may have been a little surprised and disorientated at first by this unknown piece, and looked for some point of reference. Was it an arrangement, an improvisation, a new work? And then all at once, with a big smile on his face, Schneiderhan carried the whole of the hall with him. He gave a charming wink to the audience and began tapping his feet. As if they had been given permission to let their hair down, the officers immediately joined in, beating the ground with their boots. The others clapped their hands in rhythm. The Mozarteum echoed with joy, with the pure love of music. A tribute! And not only to Mozart.

Stefan's whole body went stiff. He turned to me, shocked, incredulous. He had recognized the tune as soon as the first notes rang out, the old man's song, the Jewish melody. There were no Jews about anymore, not in Salzburg, and not in the countryside where he lived. They had been made to clear out, as he had said. But their music was ringing out now, right there in the Festspiele, *in the Mozarteum, driving the Nazis to distraction. Carried away, I stood up to demonstrate my excitement at Schneiderhan's talent. Then, little by little, row by row, they all stood up, applauding, taking up the tune. In all that din, I murmured the words, as best I could, in Yiddish. Like a prayer. To ask forgiveness of those who had once sung it, at weddings and barmitzvahs. To ask forgiveness for this fraud.*

Am I not myself like that song? A forgery? A pot-pourri? Not completely Jewish, not really an atheist, half-Austrian, half-Silesian, not yet dead and yet still banished from the world of the living?

They didn't notice a thing. Even Hans, whom I had convinced that the tune was an old melody from the Tyrol. A gem of Teutonic folklore. Mozart would have taken it and made it his own, turned it into a sonata. It kept the old man in the sanitarium alive for a while. Now, it's given me a reprieve, a kind of remission. And now, it's also going to be running through the heads of a few German soldiers, a few SS officers, like a distant echo. A ghost.

Stefan wasn't amused. He didn't laugh, even when the audience joined in with Schneiderhan. He brought me back to the sanitarium without saying a word. All sulky. I'm afraid he'll inform on me. But isn't he an accomplice? He supplied the ink and the paper, and took me to the concert. And what about Hans? Or Schneiderhan? The Festspiele committee will never admit to such a blunder.

You see, Dieter, this rather foolish gesture, this student hoax, is destined to be my sole act of resistance. I didn't kill Hitler. Or save Mozart. But I do have the feeling that I did my duty. I just wanted to stop a voice being silenced. One voice out of many thousands, but a voice which, if it had been stifled, would have killed the music in me. And all music.

A whole oratorio is affected by the absence of a single chorus member. It sounds false in spite of the sound of the orchestra, the resonance of the tenor. The gap screams. The absence can be heard in spite of everything. Like a piano with one key missing. There is no music by default.

The Talmud says that when a man saves one soul, it is as if he had saved the whole world. I haven't saved anyone's soul, not even my sister's, or Sapperstein's. Have I even saved mine?

Not yet. I have one last task to undertake. If I have the courage. This is almost certainly the last letter I will write to you. I can only wish you a long life, a good life, and one in which you never abandon your dreams. Even if, in order to realize them, you have to turn everybody against you. I enclose a copy of the famous score. To amuse you. And in the hope that you too will sing it, in my memory.

I love you.

Dad

Saturday 20 July 1940

S tefan still angry. But I don't think he has any intention of informing on me.
  Quite tired since the concert. I'm trying to recover
my strength.

Monday 22 July 1940

  The little old man's bed is still unoccupied. In the other
wards, the beds recently vacated have also remained
empty. The sanitarium doesn't seem to be admitting any
new patients. Wounded soldiers, on the other hand, arrive
every day.

  I get down to writing my last article as a music critic, but
I have no spare paper to make a fair copy. And I don't want
any prescription sheets. One of my neighbors in the ward has
promised to buy me some the next time he goes into town.

Tuesday 23 July 1940

  Stefan came. He looked embarrassed. He just gave me
a brief nod and started dismantling the old man's bed. I
didn't dare speak to him, but another patient asked him
what he was planning to do with it. Stefan replied that he

was taking it down to the second floor along with all the other unoccupied beds from the third floor. For the soldiers. There are so many of them that some will have to sleep in the corridors.

Thursday 25 July 1940

These days the nurses just rush in, hastily hand out medicines, and rush out again. The meals are becoming more and more liquid, gruel, mash, soft cheese. They are already cold by the time Stefan brings them up. We have to take the food in bowls to those who can no longer get out of bed. The dirt is piling up. It's unbearable, especially in the toilets. No more toilet paper, only old newspapers. Which I don't read.

And to think I was in the Mozarteum a mere week ago! It feels more like ten years. I've kept my ticket in the pocket of my pajamas. To be sure I didn't dream it. That old Jewish tune is still nagging at me. I try to hum Bach or Schubert, but that damned little song comes back to attack me as soon as I fall silent. Especially at night.

Friday 26 July 1940

My neighbor brought me some letter paper. It was all he could find. I try to make sure my handwriting is legible. I already have three copies ready. I need five in the hope that at least one magazine will agree to print my article. Which ought to cause a sensation. It's an open letter to the gauleiter, although signed with a false name, in which I protest at the choice of pieces in the second concert. Yiddish music! *Klezmer* violin! And our soldiers joining in, right there in the Mozarteum! How shameful for the fcstival, for Salzburg, for the whole of the Reich. If the Americans find out about it, they'll laugh their heads off. Maybe they'll turn it into a Broadway musical! We might as well play Mahler while we're about it. Or Mendelssohn!

Saturday 27 July 1940
Concert at the Festspielhaus. Extracts from Wagner operas. Quite pleased to be confined to bed. Hard to breathe.

Sunday 28 July 1940
False alarm. A fit of choking. As it's Sunday, a patient went to tell Stefan who brought me some hot tea mixed with schnapps. I could only get down one or two mouthfuls.

Stefan stayed with me, sitting on the edge of my bed. He gave me a cloth because I was coughing a lot and needed to wipe my mouth. He washed my forehead with warm water. It felt good, having him take care of me. Having him break my solitude. And then the attack passed.

Stefan left late in the afternoon. He rolled the cloth into a ball and ran out in a hurry. But I could see that the cloth, which he had under his arm, was stained with blood.

I'm cxhausted. Dazed. As if someone had punched me in the face.

Monday 29 July 1940
Stefan came with the doctor, who examined me for a long time. He didn't need to deliver his diagnosis. He gave me an injection as a matter of form.

*

Closing concert of the *Festspiele*. Beethoven's Eighth, more Wagner and, to finish, a symphony by Brahms. I don't remember which one. I think it's Furtwängler who'll conduct the Philharmonic.

Blood on my pajamas.

Tuesday 30 July 1940

I remember the army, my first leave, before the fighting intensified. It was in spring. Mother took me to a lovely tearoom. I was proud to be wearing my uniform. She asked after Fritz Jürgen, a school friend who was serving in the same battalion as myself. I didn't want to lie. Fritz had fallen in the early days of the war. On a mine-clearing patrol. So I answered with this stupid sentence, this pure cliché: "For him, the war is over."

*

I think Stefan came to see me while I was asleep. When I woke up, I found a piece of saveloy and two slices of bread in a paper bag. I gave them to my neighbor.

Wednesday 31 July 1940

Lovely day. From my bed, I can see the tops of the trees swaying gently in the breeze.

Friday 2 August 1940

Received rent.

Salzburg was a mecca for Nazi cultural life and a symbol of the influence of the Reich.

None of the musicians and conductors mentioned in Otto's diary ever made a stand for freedom of expression or gave the slightest aid to their persecuted colleagues. After the war, they all enjoyed the unreserved admiration of the world's music lovers.

Today, Salzburg remains one of the capitals of music and art. And the *Festspiele* still takes place every summer.

ABOUT THE AUTHOR

Raphaël Jerusalmy was born in Montmartre, France in 1954. After receiving diplomas from the École Normale Supérieure and the Sorbonne, he worked with Israeli military intelligence. He currently sells antique books in Tel Aviv.